D0567034

Waterwoman

Waterwoman

LENORE HART

BERKLEY BOOKS, NEW YORK

B

A Berkley Book
Published by The Berkley Publishing Group
A division of Penguin Putnam Inc.
375 Hudson Street
New York, New York 10014

This is an original publication of The Berkley Publishing Group.

PRINTING HISTORY
Berkley hardcover edition / June 2002

Visit our website at
www.penguinputnam.com

Library of Congress Cataloging-in-Publication Data

Hart, Lenore.
    Waterwoman / Lenore Hart.
        p. cm.
    ISBN 0-425-18471-4
    1. Virginia—Fiction.   2. Barrier islands—Fiction.   3. Sisters—
Fiction.   I. Title.

PS3608.A786 W38 2002
813'.6—dc21

                                                                    2002018256

PRINTED IN THE UNITED STATES OF AMERICA

10   9   8   7   6   5   4   3   2   1

In memory of
NANCY HENRICHSON GRONBACH,
generous friend.

*Sorrow does not leave us
where it found us
but forever changed.*

Acknowledgments

My thanks to Susan Allison and Leslie Gelbman, for understanding it all perfectly; Janet Peery and Sheri Reynolds, for generosity and vigilance and care; Brooks Miles Barnes, Eastern Shore historian *par excellence*; David Bell and Chris Wilson, for advising on details of the watermen's trade; Lisa Carrier, Doris and Noel Galen, Frank Green, Luisa Carino Igloria, and Katherine McDonald, for comments only perceptive readers can give; Susan Morey, for being a repository of good ghost stories; the workshops of the MFA Creative Writing Program of Old Dominion University, for support and suggestions; and my husband, David Poyer—first reader, best friend—for everything else. *Ex nihilo nihil fit.*

Waterwoman

Lenore Hart

Lie back, daughter, let your head
be tipped back in the cup of my hand.
Gently, and I will hold you. Spread
your arms wide, lie out on the stream
and look high at the gulls. A dead-
man's-float is face down. You will dive
and swim soon enough where this tidewater
ebbs to the sea. Daughter, believe
me, when you tire on the long thrash
to your island, lie up, and survive.
As you float now, where I held you
and let go, remember when fear
cramps your heart what I told you:
lie gently and wide to the light-year
stars, lie back, and the sea will hold you.

—"First Lesson"
by Philip Booth

One

We always had our differences, my sister and I, but I never meant to hurt her. I surely never wished her dead. Though sometimes, late at night, when I'm sitting here by her bedside, I wonder. Because in my twenty years of living, I believe I've received more than one omen of where love, hate, and rivalry has finally taken us, now that we're both grown women.

For instance, that one fall day in 1906, when Rebecca was three and I was seven. Dad had roused us early, in the yellow-gray light before dawn. He'd clumsily bundled us up as we yawned and complained, stuffed cold biscuits in our hands, and put us aboard his work boat, an old bar cat with a green sail.

"Your mam's sickly today," he told us. "Needs her rest. So you squits'll have to come along with me, God help us."

I'd never before in my life heard him use a curse word or take the Lord's name in vain, but I was too thrilled to be shocked. "Oh, yes," I shouted. "Yes, please, Dad."

Rebecca only squealed and hopped around. I was sure she was too young to grasp the rare privilege of finally being allowed what I'd thought then all little girls dreamed of: to ride along on Dad's work, to sit in the stern wearing a cap like a real waterman.

But we hadn't gotten far, only to the channel between our island and the next, when I turned to see my sister's red coat, her wool leggings, her patent shoes disappearing over the side. She dropped without a sound. The vanishing clothes were so unexpected a sight, a bewitched moment passed before I recalled Rebecca was inside them. And that she couldn't swim a lick.

I looked quick to my father, to see what he'd do about it. He was fiddling with the sail, his back to us, and hadn't seen. For yet another moment I couldn't speak; couldn't even recall Rebecca's name or my own. All I could think to do was scream. Dad dropped his line and turned to look. "What, Annie?" he said. Sharp-edged worry creased his forehead.

"Becca," was all I could get out. So I pointed over the water behind us.

Back in our wake a flailing arm, a last billow of bright red material. That was all.

He came about sharp, and in a moment we were at the spot where she'd vanished. He rushed to one side of the boat then the other, looking down. I leaned over the stern, and saw her there below. About a foot down, her face turned up to the sky, eyes open. She hung suspended in the water, trailing a string of bubbles like oversized pearls, hair a dark cloud around her face, as graceful as one of the water sprites in my fairy book. Beyond her lay the dull moon-rubble of an old oyster bed. To me it looked as if Rebecca were rising to the surface. Coming to me, not falling away. A mermaid about to be born.

My father shoved me out of the way, pushed the tiller over to head us into the wind, and jumped in. He came up with my sister clutched in one arm and hauled himself into the boat with the other. Laid her on the thwarts and turned her head, and did things to help her cough up water. At last he sat her up and wrapped her shivering body in his oilskin jacket.

Then he spanked me.

I understood why. It would have done no good to say I hadn't seen it happen; that the first I'd known of it was the sight of her legs disappearing suddenly over the side, any more than it would have helped to lie and claim I hadn't seen a thing. At seven, with Mam sick all the time, I had long since understood that my sister was my responsibility.

I endured the punishment without crying. Anyway, Dad generally had a lighter hand than Mam. Then he made me sit beside my sister.

"You're not to let go of her, maid. Not ever. She's not got the sense to look after herself yet."

I wouldn't look at him, but I nodded.

"You swear it, now?"

"Yes, Dad."

He seemed satisfied then, and went back to the tiller. Rebecca leaned into me and stopped sobbing long enough to glance up, her dark lashes clumped and spiky with tears and saltwater.

"All wet, Annie," she said, plucking at her sodden clothes. She shivered again.

I waited until my father turned away to hoist the sail before I risked giving her a light pinch. I frowned down at her, then made a big point of looking away.

Dad came about directly and headed home again. He squinted into the risen sun and muttered something like, "Mend blasted nets on such a God-given day."

Rebecca pressed closer and took my hand. When I felt hers curl like a small, cold starfish around mine, I relented and hugged her tight against me, astonished at how easily she'd almost been lost. But I still felt aggrieved. Her weight seemed to settle on my shoulders like dropped anchor chain. How long would it be before she had any good sense? It seemed hard that, until that day, I was supposed to look out for her.

Some of these winter nights now, after I've cleared the table and put away the dishes, I sit by Rebecca's bed. I sip hot tea with a little of the shine whiskey our friend Sam Doughty brings, and listen to be sure my sister's breathing is easy. If she's awake, I talk of the things we'll do when she's well. I remind her of the mischief and pleasure we found as kids, like that time I once cut all my hair off to try to be a boy. Or the way she used to always drop a ball in my lap when I was reading, to get me to come out and play.

And though it's the one story I never tell, I wonder if she ever remembers as far back as that accident in the old bar cat—the first time she nearly drowned. Or what she recalls of the night six months ago, when we fled this island and tried to outrun a storm in a motor launch.

Worse than the great nor'easter of 1897, is what I hear folks are claiming now. That one was three years before my birth, so I couldn't say. This last storm tried its damnedest to flatten our little islands, though, and the rest of the Virginia coast. No doubt they'll soon be calling it the great nor'easter of 1920, and make their children and grandchildren yawn with repeated tellings.

From the water it's easy to see the damage. But you have to walk away from the house here on Yaupon, over the dunes to the seaside, to find the sandy plot we keep for our dead. A body can count a good many more crosses there now than three months ago. We haven't put a marker out for Nathan. Not yet. Some days, though, I have gotten as far as planning one.

It'll be wood, like the others. But I picture his differently. Carved with a seabird, or maybe a curved, leaping fish. That would make Reverend Scarborough happy; he needn't know it's not the sign of Christ. But it's all Rebecca's decision, when she's feeling better. This time I won't insist on having things my own way. I understand now what it costs a body to be set on getting what you want, no matter what.

Our little island is only about a mile across. It seemed wide when I was a child, and the only place that could ever be home. We didn't know much of anywhere else then. Even now, being twenty and fully grown, I don't feel the need to, either. The buy boats that take my catch are the same ones that bought up the fish and crabs and oysters my father pulled from the water. He explained to me once that they sold them again to people in New York and New Jersey. And yet, he said, folks there sometimes went hungry and begged on the streets. It had to do with banks and markets, and sometimes business was poor.

Those lean times we ate more of the fish and crabs ourselves, but even a lazy man would be hard put to go hungry on the Eastern Shore. We still have no electricity, but ducks and muskrats and other game crowd the woods and shore. You can grow anything green most of the year, and there's always the water, full of crab and shrimp and mananose clams. All that city business seemed far away to us then. It still does now.

I'm the sister who was never much to look at, even as a baby, when most are at least passably cute. But until I went to school, mainly just my folks saw me growing up on Yaupon Island, and Granny Jester and my little sister Becca. So I was a happy child with a coming appetite, and gave no thought to good looks or what they might mean to a girl in this world.

I didn't know any better than to stay happy for a long time. Didn't know there might be more than what all we had. And then, when I finally discovered something to hunger after, it hadn't a thing to do with banks or cities or even electric-powered gadgets. Some days I believe it was my selfishness and greed that brought calamity down on us, just like Mam and Granny Jester said I would. Other days, I know it was only bad judgment and bad weather.

I don't have much to fear losing now, but I intend to hang on. What's left is all the more precious to me. I intend to spend the rest of my natural life free of envy and spite and the bother of love, or what passes for it in most folks' minds. As vain a wish as any human could make, I guess. But I aim to give it a go, nonetheless. I told Rebecca that just the other day, and it got a smile out of her. She knows me well enough not to be impressed.

Two

I'd just turned four the day my baby sister arrived, and she was a big surprise to me. People didn't talk to children about having babies, so Mam's growing stomach hadn't meant a thing. Mam had had a boy baby twelve years before she birthed me, but he was sickly from the get-go. One morning before he'd even learned to walk, they found him cold and blue in his crib. He's buried on the far side of the island, though high tide and storms have scoured the poor tyke's resting place into naught but a smooth blanket of sand and sea grass. After he died, years passed, and until I came along Mam and Dad had about given up on children.

The first I knew of Rebecca was a fast sail in the early dawn to the Eastern Shore town of Wachapreague, me grumbling and cold and put out that I had to leave my bed so early and no breakfast to boot. Mam sat beside me in

Dad's oyster boat, hunched over on the seat, moaning as if something was hurting her. But I was only a child and all I could think of was the injustice done my empty belly.

A horse and wagon took Mam away at the dock. Dad walked me over to eat at a place with oilcloth-covered tables and little ruffled calico curtains and a huge black woman in a flowered dress and apron who put food silently on the table and then disappeared into the back. My first restaurant meal, but the thrill was lost on me.

"Who is that woman? Why do they need five tables to eat?" I asked Dad. "Where are all her children? How many does she have?"

He wasn't eating his fried ham, just sipping coffee and looking worried.

"Never you mind, Annie," he said. "It's your mother gone to Canaan, is all, and the midwife's fee high as quinine. What a time to drop one. Look at the wind change, now! Weather's going to haul about sundown. Be a tickly bender crossing that water to carry us all home."

I frowned into my scrambled eggs. "Mam's gone where?" Suddenly an idea seized me, and I burst into tears. "She's not going to die like old Tab?"

I'd found our orange cat stiff under the porch the week before. Mam told me Tab had worked hard and done her duty with the mice, and now she'd gone to Glory. I had an idea Canaan might be the same place.

"She's not *gone*," he said. "See, a baby—"

Dad stopped and I noticed his face was red. "Just gone off a little while, to get you a surprise. You'll see, bimeby."

Hours later, I was wrapped in a spare sail, nodding off in our boat. Then I recall opening my eyes to see my father smiling at me as he handed a shaky-looking Mam down off the pier and onto the bobbing deck. "Well, what d'you think of your new sister, Annie Revels?" he asked.

"I didn't ask for no baby," I said to the wrinkled, red, squalling thing Mam held out to show me. My mother looked thin and tired, her cheeks ghost-hollow.

"A sister is better than anything," she said.

"Aye, but we could use a son," my father said, and he spat over the side.

I wasn't convinced either. "Send it back to the store. I'd rather have a kitten."

But to my annoyance neither of my parents took to that idea, and baby Rebecca rode in a clothes basket in Dad's oyster boat all the way from the mainland. The weather, as it often does on the Shore, had changed again. We had a calm trip back to Yaupon Island.

After we came home, Mam went straight to bed. In the days that followed it seemed she had a hard time just to get up and cook a little dinner or even walk out to the privy. She didn't pay any attention to me except when I brought drawings bunched in my fist to her bed. Then she'd only raise her head to look over the bundle that was my sister nursing at her breast. Mam always smiled weakly at my pictures but otherwise ignored the scrawled cats and toys I'd meant as a further hint of things I considered a better deal than a baby. And little Rebecca was fretful, fussing at all hours, getting up all times of the night to nurse and wail, then nurse some more. I slept with a pillow over my head, sorry to be afflicted with a sister at all.

After three weeks of this, Dad went off and came back with Granny Jester. She'd visited twice before and spoiled me with a bag of sugar cookies and a new tin pail and shovel. She looked like an older version of Mam, wore the same steel-rimmed spectacles, her hair still as black as the stripe on a gull's wing.

She looked at baby Rebecca, wrapped like a batch of fresh biscuits in a clean tea towel.

"Well, ain't you gussed up," said Granny, laughing as she peered down at Rebecca's blue eyes and pink pursed mouth, her waving fists that poked from the towel. The first thing Gran did was gather up a load of wash, so the baby could have a proper blanket, one of my old ones. My father had brought us a new gasoline-powered wringer washer in the boat along with Granny. He lugged it out back to the shed and made a big production of setting it up, fussing and shaking his head and clanging tools, but looking proud afterward.

"What a racket," I shouted, holding my ears as he turned it on to show off its features. He said no one else hereabouts but for the hotel over at Cobb's Island had an automatic washer, and I should be grateful. I thought about that a while but still couldn't see why. The house used to be quiet, except when I'd played at cowboys or hopscotch and intended to make noise. Now there were not one but two noisy additions I had never wanted or asked for.

After dinner that night, Mam went straight to bed. As I sat under the kerosene lamp, drawing a picture on an old piece of butcher paper, I heard Granny Jester whisper across the table to Dad, "Oh, George. She has broke since the last time I saw her."

I looked around. Did she mean me? She must mean Mam, I finally decided. But my mother wasn't broken, like the wooden horse Dad had whittled for me, then stepped on early one morning because I'd left it out in the hall. No, Mam was not broken; but I had seen that each day baby Rebecca took what strength she had in her and sucked it right up.

Granny Jester said she was there to help with the baby, but I decided she was really there to play with me. After the housework was done she took me for walks around the island. We picked up shells and sea glass, and she let me climb up in bed with her morning and night. She read to me out of the big book of fairy stories kept on the bedroom shelf. Though I noticed she sometimes changed the endings, so that little girls who trod on a loaf or danced themselves nearly to death in red shoes or got eaten by wolves didn't perish at all. They only repented and became good children who minded their table manners, instead of going footless ever after or being roped to a moldy old hunk of bread for eternity.

Gradually I resented Rebecca not so much. Her face grew less red and wrinkled, and she even smiled at me from time to time. I began to look at her with some affection. But Mam didn't get much better.

"Have some more of this Hog Island chowder," Gran would say. "Or one of my good sweet potato biscuits."

"No thanks, Mother. I've run ashore," Mam would usually answer, though she'd hardly had a bite, handing whatever it was to me or Dad to finish.

She was out of bed by then but mostly sat around and stared out the window, the baby at her breast, waiting for Dad to get home off the water. She seemed to have forgotten how to do the simplest things, like boil water for coffee or make my oatmeal in the mornings.

So Granny stayed on, and after a while it seemed she had always been with us. After a while more, the baby was crawling and eating her oatmeal, too, but still Mam sat and sighed, and sometimes got dressed and sometimes didn't. When she did get up she only stayed in a chair, head tucked down, hands folded in her lap. Or gazed out the window as if she were waiting for the sight of something she knew would never really come. It scared me when I thought about it. Hard to remember that she used to play at building towns with the blocks Dad had cut and carefully sanded for me. That, once in a while, if I begged and teased for it, she used to even take off her shoes and hopscotch across the floor.

I decided that if the baby had taken all the play out of the mother I had known, at least I had Gran. She was mine, and I wasn't going to share her with anyone. Least of all a baby sister who already gobbled up more than her share.

The months passed, and one winter morning, I lay in bed with Granny Jester. She had finished braiding my hair and was reading to me. I noticed, out of the corner of my eye, that Rebecca was up, too. She spotted us through the open door, looked delighted, and crawled around the corner and over the threshold.

I watched her progress across the rag rug toward the bed. She cooed some of her pigeon sounds and stared up at me. Granny didn't seem to notice; but then she was a bit hard of hearing. I closed my eyes and wished Rebecca away. This was my time; Gran was mine. And anyway, my sister had Mam.

" 'The better to see you with, my dear,' " Gran growled in the deep voice I always begged her to do for the wolf. "And then the maiden said to the beast dressed in the poor old woman's clothes, 'But Grandmother! What big ears you have.' "

Rebecca grabbed the hem of the quilt in her chubby fists. I watched in alarm as she began to haul herself upright. In a moment, she'd be in the bed with us. She'd take Granny Jester for herself, too. I glanced at my grandmother, but she was reading on and still seemed not to have noticed the baby.

So I carefully slid my leg across the sheet, and from under the covers gave Rebecca a nudge with my foot, just a little one to make her get down. I must have startled her, because she let go of the covers and fell back. At first she only plopped down hard on her diapered bottom, looking stunned. But then she went on over, and her head hit the leg of the bedside table.

I glanced away from my howling sister and up into Granny's shocked face, staring down as if she didn't know me. Then she shoved me aside, got up and gathered Rebecca to her, feeling my sister's chubby arms and legs for some injury. For all the fuss she was making, I expected blood, but there was none I could see. Yet Granny looked at me over the baby's head as if I'd tried to murder her.

"Cain slew Abel," she said to me in a hateful voice. I frowned because for a moment I didn't understand; then I remembered she'd told me that Bible story the Sunday before, after I had refused to sit next to Rebecca in the pew at church. But before I could say anything, Gran leaned over and slapped my face.

"A selfish child brings misery to a house," she said. "You're one of the blue hen's chickens, you are. Mayhap you'll grow up selfish, too, eh, girl? Of a mind, I should switch you seven ways from Sunday."

She didn't, though. And when my father came in to see what all the fuss was, she only said the baby had fallen down.

But I knew she didn't look at me quite the same after that. I had reveled in being her favorite, Gran's girl. Now I was sure she didn't act the same with me. I'd look up from my plate at supper to see her gazing on me, sort of appraising, as if wondering who I really was. I tried hard to be kind with my little sister after that, but it tried me sorely. She was at the age when she would snatch up the few toys I had and drool and gum at them until they looked a terrible sight.

I had a doll, a rag one Gran had sent two Christmases earlier. In truth, I was never much for dolls, and could have given it to Rebecca without remorse. I thought about doing just that. Except she wanted it so, I looked at it with new eyes and felt it must be of greater value than I'd noticed before. Besides, if she got hold of it, then she'd have a doll and I'd have none.

Worst of all was the suspicion that Gran had told Mam on me, after all. For now it seemed to me that Mam spoke more sharply than ever before if I took more than one cookie from the jar or didn't speak sweetly enough to the baby. Gran had betrayed me, I decided, had secretly turned my mother against me, too. It was bitter to go from beloved princess to wicked girl all in a moment. I still listened to Gran's stories but sat stiffly upright instead of leaning into her. I would go quietly to the door of my parents' bedroom some afternoons, gaze at my mother's tired face pressed against the crumpled linen of her worn pillowcase, and feel sharp-edged grief. As if she were not simply sleeping but dead to me.

Then one morning, after fixing us all a good breakfast of biscuits and sausage with cream gravy and running two loads of laundry out to the shed, Granny Jester got sick. She'd seemed fine until she fell out just before noontime on the front porch, her mouth twisted all funny to one side. Dad wasn't home. So Mam, who had made an extra effort and gotten dressed that morning, somehow managed to drag and pull her to the bed in the small room off the kitchen. It had once been the pantry, but they'd made it into a bedroom when Granny arrived.

Dad got back an hour later, then turned around and went right back out in the skiff for a doctor. There was one in Exmore who would sometimes come out to the islands to see folks when they couldn't make it in. After he arrived, he shook his head over Gran and said she'd likely never get out of the bed again.

"Stroke," he said, snapping his black leather bag shut. "May talk again. Or she won't."

After that, Mam had to drag herself around and take care of the baby and her old mother who'd come to help. She still looked shadowy, thin, and sad, but she was up again, cooking and tending to the house. I wondered if somehow Granny Jester had traded places with her, had taken sick so that my mother could be well and get up again.

One morning Dad said, "For God's sake, pace yourself. Needn't run in at any little noise. She's not a child."

But Mam only said, "If I don't turn to, I won't finish before nightfall," and went on slowly but steadily washing, feeding, cleaning, hanging up diapers large and small, and lots of soiled sheets. She was short with me, too, snapping when I spilled something or made any mess, saying Granny was right; I was her selfish girl, the bad one sent to bring her grief.

After Granny Jester was awake again and eating a little, I carried a picture book in to her. In a fit of generosity, I had decided she'd enjoy reading to me again and that I would even snuggle up as I used to. She didn't have to get out of the bed for that. I held up the book, but she closed her eyes and turned away. Mam came in carrying medicine and shooed me outside to play. When I tried again the next day, Gran made mad grunting noises, then turned a terrible face on me, worse than a goblin in a picture book. I stared, too scared for a moment to move. Then I dropped my book and ran.

Later, she took to throwing plates of food at the wall and sometimes kicking her makeshift bedpans full of piss onto the floor. Mam cleaned up without a complaint, even when Granny said bad words at her, words I'd be switched for if they ever passed my lips. Even with all Mam's scrubbing, Gran's room smelled bad after a while, a sour stink of sick and old food and creeping mildew. I heard her scream out sometimes in the middle of the night, or grunt like an animal as she used the pan my mother brought for her to do her business in.

One day I heard a terrible commotion and came to the kitchen to see what had happened. It was lunchtime, and the crash that'd brought me running was Gran hurling a bowl of soup at my mother. Broken crockery lay all around. The mess ran down the wall and puddled on the floor. Mam just stood in Granny's doorway calmly, broth and bits of vegetables dripping down the front of her skirt.

"Now, Mother, don't go up a gum like this," she pleaded. "You'll make yourself sick."

As I clung to Mam's hand, staring, Granny's gaze shifted to fasten on me. She pointed and screamed out some sounds, words I couldn't understand, and for the first time I was truly terrified of her. When I looked up, I saw my mother was crying silently, hopelessly, not making any effort to wipe her eyes, and I forgot how frightened I'd been. Mam's nose was red, leaking snot like a child's. I thought, *How dare Gran make my mam cry?*

I closed my eyes to blot out Granny's twisted, red face, the cords raised like taut fishing lines on her neck. When I opened them again, I knew what it was she reminded me of.

"You wicked old witch," I shouted.

Then, appalled at my own foolhardiness, I hid my face in my mother's apron. I felt her hand on my shoulder, but she didn't shake or smack me for sassing an adult. Just rested it lightly there a moment, then gave me a pat.

By the time I dared look again, Granny Jester's face had gone from mottled red to an ugly purple.

"George, come quick," my mother called. Then she shoved me toward the door. "Go get your father."

I dashed out, shouting, and Dad came running from the garden. By then, Gran had collapsed, quiet at last. He laid a hand on the side of her throat.

"She's gone," he said, and Mam wiped her eyes and blew her reddened nose on her apron. He glanced at me, then said to my mother more quietly, "Made a die of it, she finally did."

He needn't have whispered. *Gone,* I knew by then, anyway, meant dead. Granny Jester was dead. But what was worse, I had been the cause of it.

A few days after the funeral, I came up from the beach after making castles and knocking them down all morning. I was tired and thirsty and hungry, and by the sun I knew it had to be Rebecca's nap time, so my mother could fuss over *me* for a change. I looked up at the house and saw her standing just back of the screen door, waiting for me. The afternoon light glinted off her glasses as she watched me run up the path. I gloated at the idea of having her all to myself, if only for an hour.

But as I got closer, I slowed my steps. I didn't like the

way the light made two silver ovals of her spectacles, as if she had no eyes. She didn't move or wave or call out. Just stood there behind the screen, waiting. Perhaps she was angry, perhaps I'd done something wrong.

As I dragged up to the front steps, sure I was in for it, I happened to look over at the side yard. There in the sun stood my mother, hanging freshly washed diapers out to dry on the line strung from the shed to the house.

"You're not Mam," I whispered to the shape behind the screen door.

It was Gran. I could see all the way through her now, clear to the wall behind where Dad's hats hung on pegs. I screamed and ran around the house to my mother. Grabbed her tight around the knees until she staggered, and hugged her so hard she scolded me for almost knocking her down.

That night, my parents put me to sleep in their room. The next week, when they tried to move me into the room where Granny had slept, and put the baby in my tiny old bedroom next to them, I hollered and cried until I burned with a fever. So they laid me in their own bed and moved Rebecca into her wicker basket on the dresser again.

For years I hated that back room, the one Granny died in, the smallest and darkest in the house. After she died, we only used it for storage and as an extra pantry again. Later, when Rebecca was older, Dad built on a bigger bedroom for us to share. He said it was easier than adding on to the sagging kitchen end, but I noticed that he and Mam rarely went into Granny Jester's old room either. Or when they had to, to find balls of string or empty packing boxes or canned vegetables, they always hurried back out again.

I used to imagine Granny still lay in there, sometimes, her spirit still angry, yet with no strength to lift the latch. But old ghosts will always find a way out.

Three

When Rebecca and I were little, I used to wake before first light, that time of day when the air is still and cool and damp, even in summer, when you live on an island. My sister usually slept later, thumb plugged in her rosy mouth, breathing softly in her cradle next to my cot. When she got older, she had the cot and I got a long, narrow rope bed with a carved wooden head- and footboard Dad brought out of storage. It seemed grand to me, a bed for a princess. Every morning but Sunday, no matter how early I ever woke, I could lie quiet and warm under my quilts and hear my father in the kitchen, poking at the hot coals in the stove or scraping the coffeepot across its cast-iron lid.

Like all watermen, he was up and out before dawn, usually by four, though he never went by a watch. I could hear his footsteps thud the planks in the kitchen, hear him mumbling to old Chester, having a regular conversation with that half-blind black Lab mutt, though he didn't talk much to anyone else, even Mam.

Less often, I'd hear her in there, too, fixing him a pan of eggs or hotcakes and homemade sage sausage, but mostly he got up on his own. Some mornings I woke to the crisp, meaty smell of black duck or a quartered muskrat frying in the black iron skillet. It was Dad taught me to cook, not Mam.

After Gran died, my mother took to her bed a good deal of the time again, so Dad let her sleep in. On bad days, she couldn't get up anyhow. She suffered often from migraines and stomach pains. Her back had gotten twisted somehow when she labored with Rebecca, and sometimes she could barely stand upright.

So I'd creep into the kitchen quietly, careful not to wake my sister as I left my bed. If I could manage to get there quietly enough, not step on the two coffered floorboards that always squeaked underfoot, this would be my time with Dad. The only time, when he wasn't outside mending nets or scraping barnacles, that he was in a mood to talk.

"Here you be, maid," he'd say, sliding a plate of fried meat or eggs and toast in front of me. "Throw that into your maw."

And I would go to work eating up his good cooking, feeling like the favored child. For I wanted to be his favorite, wanted more than anything to be like him. But the fact remained that I was a girl and just beginning to understand that I couldn't—or at least wasn't supposed to—do certain things. But I still wanted to go out on the water with him, and sometimes when Mam was tired or crying, he would give in and take me out in the boat.

I'd asked him more than once to teach me to net fish and tong for oysters. Sometimes he'd humor me, then gently untangle my fingers from the snarled net, or keep his hands firmly on my shoulders to make sure my scarecrow dance with the huge wooden tongs didn't send me overboard.

But mostly he laughed at my notions.

"Aye, I'll teach you to be a waterman, Annie Revels, and then what? Sure as gun's iron you'd get you a fellow and take off with him."

"I wouldn't," I'd cry, all indignant even before I was sure exactly what he meant by it. At six I rarely ever saw any boys, except on trips to the Methodist church on Hog Island, and then they were all slicked up and unnaturally quiet in a hard wooden pew, looking like muskrats in a trap. I couldn't imagine playing with a boy, much less "running off" with one, whatever that meant. Anyway, where would I run to? This was home.

"Oh, aye, you would," he'd reply, looking at me and squinting hard, jaw thrust out. "It's no fault of yours, maid. That's as it's meant to be. Sure, we could have used a son, but girls don't belong out here. Women and water? That's black gum against thunder."

So I learned more of cooking from him, mornings, than

I did of fishing. Dad's favorite dish was muskrat, maybe because it was a change from the taste and smell of fish and oysters.

"Give me ary arster or a nice fried panfish. But I can't abide crab no more. I've already et my fill of them on earth," he'd say, and he didn't care to have another morsel.

So it was my father, George Revels, who taught me you had to soak a fresh pair of muskrats overnight in salt water before you dredged them in flour and salt and pepper and fried them in lard. Mam couldn't make decent muskrat; hers came out tough as whitleather. Dad made the best gravy from drippings, too. But he was up so early and sometimes out so late, he didn't spend much time in the kitchen except in the morning.

I had to take over the cleaning and cooking early on. I hated sweeping up and slapping heavy, wet laundry into the basket and hauling it out to the line. I liked to make food, but I hated being tied to the house. By the time I was eight, I was doing right much of the chores. Rebecca was so much younger she couldn't help out at first. She only played.

She liked dolls. Once she saw one at the E. L. Willis Store in Willis Wharf, a china baby with dark for-real hair, in a lace christening gown. But Dad thought store-bought was mostly a waste, especially such useless things as play-pretties. When she found out she wasn't going to get it, she howled all the way back to the boat.

The next day, Dad made her a nice jointed one out of

clear pine. By the time she was five, she was fixing up doll clothes from sewing scraps. Still, she was never satisfied with the homemade one. Mostly it lay on her cot, dressed in her latest effort at doll fashion. When she got older, she'd spend hours fussing with Mam's long hair, so much like her own. She would unbraid and brush it over and over, till it shone like yards of dark silk spread across the pillow. Then she'd braid it up all over again, making such fancy loops and twists all over Mam's head, a cat would have laughed to see them.

But sometimes Rebecca and I got along fine. When she got old enough to walk and talk, I liked to roll a ball to her, or play ring-around-the-rosy, because she laughed so hard every time I fell down, and then she'd fall on top of me. It surprises me now, when I think of all the silly things we liked. Going barefoot all summer, and playing fifty-oh. One of us would go off and hide, while the other would cover her eyes, then be the finder.

It was me taught her how to play cat's cradle with bits of old line or Mam's leftover yarn. Becca would sit between my outstretched legs, leaning back against me. I'd hold my arms out and work the patterns up close so she could catch on. Now and again she'd look up, eyes wide, and grin at me as if I were the greatest thing going. Those times I was thankful to have a little sister and tried to be careful with her. Mam said I had to be kind, and a good example, though she never did explain exactly what-all that meant.

But the older I got, the more I wanted to be out in the

boat with Dad. The few times I did go on the water with him, I saw men and their sons—hardly older than me—working side by side. Yes, and grandfathers, too. This was after Rebecca was born, and Dad took charge of me sometimes to ease Mam's burden and give Granny some peace. Those are still my best recollections of him.

There was no longer much use by then to try dredging oysters from the small bays and deep channels. They'd been long since fished out. But a while before I was born the state had decided to lease some of the best grounds, and Dad was wise enough not to bicker and sulk about rights and freedom as some had done. Instead, he paid up and got first choice. Then he'd seeded the barren old beds with shells and some live oysters. They'd spawned, and soon he had thriving nurseries with bushels of shellfish.

But the times he took me out it was mostly after crabs. We'd check the pots first, in the winding tide channels that threaded the sea-fronting marshes. Then he'd sail out to lay down a trotline, letting me help pay it out over the stern, a run of woven cotton at least a quarter-mile long, baited with chunks of salted eel. Eel is the only bait for crabs.

I learned that one day when we finished laying the trotline and doubled back. We came on a small, idling motorboat. The man standing in it had a big galvanized bucket at his feet and held a ball of what looked like clothesline.

Dad asked what he thought he was doing. The man, who

was sunburned and dressed in a suit vest but wore no shirt, said he was laying a trotline.

Dad shifted his chew to one cheek. "What business you in?" he asked, as if he were interested. "What's your bait?"

The man grinned. He had a strange accent. "Me? Insurance binness in Jersey. Bought a little camp at Wachapreague. Bait's chicken necks, what else." The fellow looked sure of himself then. "Everybody knows that."

Dad spat his chew over the side. "Well, honey," he said to the man, "everbody's wrong. There's only one bait for crab, and that's fresh eel, salted down. With twenty-pound number-one cotton line, like I got laid down right here. And I'll give you some more advice."

He reached under the bench seat and came up with his old shotgun. He didn't point it at the insurance man, just cradled it in one sun-freckled arm against his side.

"Don't care for any damn chicken neckers fouling my trotline just because they so dumb they can't see where it ends and where it begins."

The man in the other boat raised his hands as if warding off bad luck. "Now look here . . ."

But Dad interrupted. "Honey boy, you look what you're doing to me. Look here at this child. You going to tell me you got a permit to take the food out her mouth and the clothes off her back?"

"No, not at all," said the man, looking pale around the edges of his sunburn.

"That's good." Dad squinted up at the sky, as if his next

words were written on the clouds. "Now, I can see you're just a damn amateur chicken necker. Sometimes watermen from Maryland, they come down here and run a line. Lately they been crabbing on Sundays. Good Methodist or no, a man ought to take some rest."

The man in the boat nodded. I saw his Adam's apple bobbing, and that he was slowly reeling in and balling up the line in his hands. "Yes, that's true. Thank you," he said.

Then he turned his boat slowly, carefully, and putted away. We watched him go until he was a water-bug speck.

"Would you have shot him? That fella," I said.

My father glanced down as if surprised to see me. Then he laughed. "Course not, little knuckle-headed girl," he said, knocking lightly on the top of my head.

"Ouch," I said, though it didn't hurt. "But you took your gun out."

"When I came out here and pulled up my line tomorrow, his would've laid across it and shaken off half the crabs afore we could even snatch up a dip net. And then we'd go without. Not him. He's in *insurance*," Dad said, the way you might say, *He's a circus clown.*

"He been a waterman, though . . ." Dad looked up at the sky again, then back down at me, as if he'd just recalled I was still with him. He shook his head. "No fit place," he said. "And that's the smart of it."

Maybe I should've been shocked or frightened. But I thought it was thrilling, like something from one of my cowboy books, that my own father would take care of us no matter what, even if it meant he had to sling a gun like a desperado.

Every morning after that, when I woke and heard him stirring, I hoped he'd call up the stairs again, tell me to get a move on, get dressed, come help him load crab pots or wash the deck. But if I came down and offered, he'd only look at me over his coffee mug, shift his pipe to the other side of his mouth, and snort.

"Black gum against thunder," he'd say again and shake his head. So by that I knew that if I had been born a boy, he would have taken me in a minute.

Even though he didn't think the sea was a fitting place for women or girls, I loved everything about it, even the wild squalls that sometimes shook our house. When chores were done, I'd walk out on the marsh to watch the herons fish. Or I might tie a string around an old bone or some scrap meat, for eel was pretty dear, and drag that bait through the shallow green water, hoping an old sook or a Jimmy crab would get interested. Once they pinched a claw around their supper, they never let go, even when you popped them in the bucket.

But don't we all hang on like that and never turn loose, even when it means we're bound to be killed and eaten the next minute?

I turned eight before Dad finally sent me over to the school on Hog Island, at Broadwater. Island people don't place so much importance on education. Most everything you need to know for your living you learn outside a classroom, from your folks. Still, I could already recite my alphabet by the time I was six; Mam had taught me that much. But she wasn't inclined to do more. So Dad sailed me over to the Hog Island school most days.

I tried a couple times to talk him into letting me work with him instead.

"I could mend nets," I said. "I can bait the pots, too. And I'm not afraid of crabs." I meant not afraid to scoop them out. You can't grab one at a time when you pull pots, a mass of them all lumped together, climbing over each other, fighting and pinching. You've got to jump in with both hands and untangle as best you can.

He smiled, leaned over, and patted my knee. "That's true. Some folks are plain feared of 'em. Not you. The Lord knows they can't hurt you much."

Strictly speaking, that's not so. Crabs have good rear vision; you can't sneak up on them. I'd already had a few nasty nips from big Jimmies that made my eyes water. But I wouldn't have cried in front of Dad for anything.

He was silent for a moment, and I felt a prickle of hope. Then he shook his head. "Black gum," he said shortly and jerked at the tiller as if angry about something.

So that fall I entered the second grade, where I learned spelling, and arithmetic, and that some of the girls who sat around me in class were pretty, but I was not.

One day at recess, Tommy Kellum, an older boy in my class who was a real game-make, ran up to me on the playground. He chanted, "Birdy, birdy, Annie, Annie, looks like a heron with her skinny fanny."

All the boys and some of the girls who weren't too prim about the "fanny" part fell out all over the place laughing. I stood in the center of a circle, feeling hateful heat as my face reddened. I knew I was tall like Mam, like Granny Jester. The tallest in the class, in fact. And my hair, though thick and golden brown, was always tangled and flyaway. Mam never had the energy to brush it real good. And I had loads of freckles splotched pretty much all over. But at home none of this had mattered. I was just Annie, and I looked as Annie should.

I took a deep breath, made a fist, and knocked Tommy Kellum down. I made him cry, a big boy, and then no one ever dared to compare me to a shore bird again. But I suspected that somehow, some way, I'd still lost that fight.

The next year Rebecca began riding over in the boat, too. She was only five, young for school, but Mam was tired and sick as two dogs at the time from some female trouble; it was hard on her to have to chase after my sister all day long. So Rebecca entered the classroom behind me that fall, clinging to my oilskin jacket. I hauled her like a tugboat to an empty seat and put her into it.

Miss Hightower looked at us over her wire-rims. "Why, who's this, Annie?"

"My sister," I said, proud to be the elder one. "I have to watch out for her."

Miss Hightower got up and came around her desk. "Why, what a pretty little thing you are," she said to Rebecca. She glanced at me again. "I'd never have imagined— well, never mind. Listen, everyone," she called in a high, cheerful voice. "Give me your attention. This is Annie's little sister. You must make her welcome and be kind to her."

The whole class silently regarded her and then me. One by one, their gazes went back to Rebecca again. That day I learned that people always prefer to look at the prettiest thing in a room. That was Rebecca, for sure. She was the one with hair the fine black silk of Mam's. Her skin was soft, and since she didn't like to play outside, it was white and smooth as new-ironed linen.

At lunch that same day, when we took out our pails, Tommy Kellum made a fool of himself giving Rebecca his apple when she dropped hers in the sand. Meg Phillips, who never ever spoke to me, gave her a brand-new hair ribbon for no good reason at all. I decided that if she had crowed about it or snatched at the things they offered, you could have hated Rebecca. But she'd always smile or give a little cry of real pleasure, and then you had to smile at her, too. As did Dad and Mam. And I did, too.

In that classroom full of runny noses, sunburned cheeks,

and home-cut hair, Rebecca was like a china doll, silent and pretty and perfect. Your eyes wanted to admire her, to keep her that way just to look at.

I hadn't noticed it so much at home; we were all too used to her there. But here it was obvious. Even Miss High-tower was smitten. Maybe that's why it took her a long time to see that Rebecca would hardly ever get her letters right. That she rarely finished her arithmetic and yawned over her primer. Everyone made excuses; sometimes they even did the work for her. No matter I might sweat all evening before dinner, tongue clamped between my teeth, bent over a laborious page of cursive; the next day I knew that Rebecca's old blue hair ribbon would gather more compliments than all my pained, lengthy scribbling.

By the time I was thirteen, I got good and fed up with the laundry, the dirty dishes and all. You had to wait for a fine, clear sky to do laundry; for the kind of day that was really made for play. So one hot washing day, I ran a few loads through the machine. Rebecca hung two socks, then she wandered back inside. I kept pinning wet shirts savagely to the line, pretending the pegs were pinching my sister's soft, idle arms. I didn't want to be doing a grown woman's chores all the time, either. I wanted to be out on the water with Dad.

"Rebecca," I shouted at the house, but she didn't answer. I decided she was probably sitting on the edge of the bed, fooling with Mam's hair or her own. I tugged on a hank of my unruly wild brown flyaway stuff, but still it hung in my eyes. I yelled, "Rebecca!" again. No answer.

I went inside and peeked into Mam's room. She sat on the end of her bed, smiling as Rebecca combed and combed her hair.

"I'm making her pretty," said my sister, as if daring me to stop her from a vitally important job. It struck me then that she'd never offered to braid or brush my hair, as if she'd long ago decided it was beyond fixing.

"Well, I'm doing laundry," I said. "And you're old enough to help."

"Now Annie," said Mam reproachfully. "Becca's helping." Though she patted my hand, she frowned at me. "My two good girls," she said. But it was Becca she smiled at.

My sister looked triumphant as a creamery cat over my mother's shoulder. Suddenly I couldn't stand the sight of the two of them. I suppose I was really angry at Dad, but just then it seemed to me that Becca and Mam were the cause of all my problems. I was supposed to stay in the house and like it, too. The way they did.

I turned and stomped into the kitchen, slammed the drawers around a bit. In the middle one I saw the poultry shears lying next to the bread knife. I picked up the scissors and fit my fingers into their cold steel handles. Clicked them open and shut in the air a few times. Then I raised the dull metal blades and slowly sawed at my hair until I had chopped it off above my ears all around. I went into the rag box and got an old pair of Dad's trousers that were way too small for him. I tied them on with old line so they wouldn't slip down over my skinny hips.

In the pantry was a greasy cap I'd found washed up on the tide in a clump of spartina. Some fisherman must had let it fall overboard. I held my breath and closed my eyes as a charm against ghosts, then reached in and jerked the hat off the nail where it hung.

Rebecca screamed when she came upon me outside an hour later; her face for a moment went pale with the shock of my boyish new identity. Then she hooted with laughter until she had to hold her sides against the pain.

I didn't care.

When Dad came home and saw what a fright I'd made of myself, first he laughed, too.

"O my blessed, you'd stop an eight-day clock," he said.

Then he grabbed my arm, turned me over his knee. And though I was nearly as tall as him and hung to the ground on either side, he blistered my hide. His usually light hand walloped so hard I had bruises after, and it pained me something fierce to sit down to meals for a week. No matter, I thought. Let it hurt like all the hell torments Reverend Pennewell warned us about on Sundays. I wouldn't cry.

I was too big to spank, and of course that rankled. But it was his laughing that hurt the worst. I'd thought he'd understand. After I had cut my hair and dressed in men's clothing, looking at my tanned face and broad shoulders in the mirror in the back room, it was clear to me I'd been meant to be a boy. I was even handsome that way, I thought. Wearing Dad's pants and shirt, I had felt, for the first time in my life, comfortable in my clothes and pleased with my own reflection.

Somehow Dad seemed to get the idea that school was responsible for my wanting to be a boy. He didn't take us back after the day I cut off my hair.

"Notions," I heard him mutter as he mended net in the late-afternoon light. "Education." He spat off to the side, narrowly missing one of the half-wild black hogs we sometimes made into chops and sausage, when we could catch them.

Without school and lessons to do, I had some time to kill again. If my chores were past and the day was so hot there were no crabs out in the shallows to be netted, sometimes I went around to the sea side of the island for a change of view. I left Rebecca to tend Mam. *Let her have her own living life-size doll,* I thought. *I want none of it.*

I always checked first on the black skimmers. I admired their feather-dress, black above and white below, the colors so sure and definite. I liked to walk among the nests, which weren't proper twig ones like mainland birds build in trees, just shallow cups scooped in the sand.

The first few times I came, the adult skimmers flew at me in a storm of sharp rage and flapping feathers, as if they'd poke my eyes out. I soon discovered they were all bluff. So when they saw that didn't work, they'd crawl out of their nests and belly-flop along on the sand, dragging a leg behind them, or a wing held bent at an angle, to sucker me away from their babies. Then, after a while, they got used to me and barely turned their heads or ruffled a feather when I walked by. Like folks, they could get used to anything, if it stayed around long enough.

Sometimes I used to sit out on the beach when no one needed me in the house and look out over the water. If I was on the west shore of the island, the side the house faced, I could just make out the mainland, a smudged-charcoal line of trees. But mostly I liked to sit on the windy northeast side, where I could see over the gray-blue Atlantic water to Cobb's Island, to the roofs of its hotel and the drill pole of the Coast Guard station, its snapping flag like a colored postage stamp in the wind. Sitting there, looking out, was the only place I could still pretend I was in the boat, out on the water with Dad.

By then I knew how to do it all, I was sure, from watching him frame eel pots and mend nets. Sometimes he'd still let me dig clams or maybe chop a horseshoe crab for bait. I knew eels wanted fresh, clean meat, and that you had to use squid or live minnows to catch fluke fish. I'd watched him drag for flounder, and bet I could do it in my sleep, if he'd ever take me out.

But by then I also knew he'd never give me a chance. The joke would be on him, though, I decided, when no boy ever asked me to run off with him. My father would be stuck with me for the rest of his life, a woman without a husband who wasn't allowed to work at the only job around. And it would be his own fault. I felt brief, spiteful pleasure at the idea of causing him a bit of grief and trouble, but that wasn't nearly enough to make me feel better.

Sometimes boats loaded with sportsmen passed our island. I'd seen these for years: long, sleek, white-painted motor launches with a tanned local guide at the wheel, shepherding a gaggle of gaping women in white dresses and parasols. Or a couple of tourist men headed out to fish or shoot Canada geese or black duck. I'd heard my father talk of the Cobb's Island Hotel, a big rambling place with ells tacked on here and there.

The first Cobb had bought the island from a fisherman who had squatter's rights. Some say they gave him thirty dollars and a sack of salt for it. Then Cobb and his sons set to salvaging wrecks. They got windfall-rich when a ship from Brazil, loaded with coffee, went aground on the bar. They saved the beans and got ten thousand dollars for their trouble. So old Cobb retired from the wreckers' trade and built his hotel.

We were some sort of distant relatives of the Cobbs, Gran had once told me. Perhaps second or third cousins. I hadn't understood the convoluted genealogy she'd tried to impart between reading and playing cat's cradle, and wished now I could unravel it. Maybe they'd be willing to give a girl a chance. Surely I could steer a boat as well as any dressed-up guide. But it seemed there'd been a falling-out decades earlier, and the families never spoke after that. I tried not to feel despair at the fact that all the guides I ever saw were men who looked much older than me, anyway.

We had never visited Mr. Cobb or his sons, who should be old now, too. Sometimes I'd wave as the Cobbs' flotillas passed; skiffs and longboats and even an old skipjack or two full of tourists bristling with fishing rods and guns, as if they were bound to take on the U.S. Navy. Rowley Cobb, the old man, kept his own little catboat, and he'd sit bolt upright at the tiller, beard a yellow-white streamer in the wind. I knew that later all the launches would come back with gunwales low in the water. I saw those boats many a time weighted with more black duck than anyone could ever eat.

"Wasteful," Dad had said in disgust, when I mentioned this one night at supper. "Making a living off tourists ain't no better than whoring in Norfolk."

Still, I wondered if Mam ever wished she was on better terms with the Cobbs. Wondered if she ever wished she might have lived in a place as big and fine as their hotel, with a staff of people just to do the chores. Once on a rainy day, near crazy with boredom, I was rooting around looking for old magazines and found a piece of newsprint in a box under my parents' bed. Stained and creased, yellow with age, the thin sheet crackled in my hands. I wondered why Mam had saved it. In the self-centered way of a young girl, I assumed it had to have something to do with me.

But when I smoothed its wrinkles flat on the sand-gritty floor, this is what I read:

RESORT OPEN ALL THE YEAR LONG.
The Grandest Surf-Bathing on the Whole Atlantic Coast.
Boating, Hunting, Fishing.
The Hunter's Own Paradise.

COBB'S ISLAND HOTEL

COBB AND SPADY, PROPRIETORS,
Cobb's Island, Northampton County, Virginia

TERMS:

Per Day $2.50
Per Week 12.00
Per Month 40.00

Children under twelve years old and Servants—Half Price.

On the other side was a faded picture of a long table. Dark-skinned, broad-hipped women stood behind it, dressed in white aprons and caps, the lighting focused on the loaded table so that the only detail of their expressions I could make out was here and there a glimpse of teeth or eyeball white. I had a momentary flash of a dark-skinned, silent woman bringing me food in a room full of empty checker-clothed tables. Then it was gone, and the picture of the long dining table full of who-knew-what treasures drew me again. What sort of party could it have been—a big day, a family dinner?

I held the paper up to catch the weak afternoon sun from the window before I could credit my eyes. A whole fish, at least three feet long, on a silver tray. A cake or maybe a giant corn pone, on a glass platter the size of a cartwheel. A haunch of beef that would feed an Indian tribe. A pile of what had to be a hundred blue crabs, succulent legs needling out like spines on a porcupine. And there were more bowls and trays loaded with stuff I couldn't identify, swirled with icing, nestled in linen, something steaming like hot pudding in shiny metal urns.

It made me hungry, though we'd just eaten the noon meal, and supper was a long way off. I thought this paper must somehow be shameful, since it had been hidden away under the bed. Was this what Dad condemned the Cobbs and their tourists for? I thought perhaps it had been hidden so I would never see, that the sight of so much laid out for people just to fill their bellies, the picture of so much *waste*, might somehow ruin me. Give me notions, like education, of who knew what. I quickly slid it back under the bed, tearing it in the process, and lived in a sweat off and on for weeks that I would be dragged out of bed in the middle of the night and whipped for it, though by then I was near as tall as Dad and then some.

A lot of the crabs he trapped and the oysters he dredged went to Cobb's for tourists, though. I guess he figured their money was as good to feed his family with as any, and he didn't have to be sociable or condone their excess to take it. The rest of the peelers and soft crabs and steamer clams and flounder all went up north. The dealers on the buy boats that came down from there had told him that Yaupon Island oysters were famous even in New York City, and he liked to repeat this, but in an offhand way, as if he really didn't care.

When I was younger, I had wondered why those folks didn't go out and catch their own crabs instead. Dad told me then they didn't have time or didn't live on the water but inland where the roads were as wide as the stillwater between us and the mainland. I figured he was pulling my leg or at least exaggerating. I just couldn't feature it.

Four

Halfway through my teens, the Great War came to Europe. All it
meant to us here was that a few of the boys I'd been to
school with had to go away and fight somebody the newspapers called the evil Hun. That their families had to do
without them for a time. Sam Doughty, the quiet, dark-
haired, Hog Island boy who used to help Rebecca with her
spelling, got drafted. So did my old playground foe, Tommy
Kellum. When I heard that, it seemed to hurt me somehow,
inside. I couldn't figure that. I had never liked Tommy,
though it had seemed, back in our school days, he had been
smitten with my little sister for a while.

A few months after we'd heard this news, Dad pulled up
and came across the yard to the house, hurrying faster than
usual. He had a bundle of mail in his arms—not so much
really, for we had few outside friends and even fewer rel-

atives. I assumed it would be a catalog or two, a newspaper, and maybe something he'd ordered for the boat.

"See here, Annie," he said when I came down the front steps. He had a strange look on his face. "You got a letter. It was at the Willis Grocery when I stopped by to pick up the mail."

Well, that in itself was cause for wonder. I had used to write to a girl cousin of mine who lived off in West Virginia. But it had been years since we'd exchanged a letter.

Then Dad said in a hushed voice, "It's all the way from France."

Well, that was surely impossible. I snatched the letter from his hand, and he didn't even chide me for bad manners. I heard Rebecca come out onto the porch behind me. "What is it?" she said, touching my arm. "What you got there, Annie?"

I shook her hand off. I was trying to read the name and address on the flimsy blue tissue of the letter. That was the third surprise. It was from Private Tommy Kellum.

I held it out and showed it to her then, struck speechless.

"Oh, Annie," she cried, clapping her hands together. "You got a boyfriend. You have one, at last."

"Don't be silly," I said. "It's only Tommy Kellum." But I turned away and took the letter into the house, with Dad and Rebecca following in my wake.

"Open it, Annie," Rebecca said eagerly. "Tell us what all it says."

"All right," I agreed finally, though I really wanted to

hold it a bit longer. To enjoy the feeling of being singled out, chosen, that the first sight of it had given me. For I was sure when I opened the letter and read it, it would only hold questions about the weather, or maybe worse, even more childish schoolyard insults from Tommy.

I opened it and unfolded the single sheet inside. It was short, only a paragraph or two. I read aloud to my audience, " 'Dear Annie Bet you are surprized to hear from me, almost as surprized as I am to be writting to you here from this muddy hole in the ground in France exactly where I cant tell its not allowed.' "

The letter was full of mistakes and had not much punctuation to speak of. That was Tommy Kellum, all right. He'd often stood in the corner for his poor spelling at the Hog Island School. But when I glanced up, Dad and Becca were staring at me, as if I were a whole play all by myself. So I went on.

" 'It is not much doing here at the moment but sometimes we sit and listen to the shells whiz overhead and wonder if the next one has our name on it ha ha but seriousley I think I have gotten a real case of religion for the first time in my life. I think about how we all used to play on the school ground it seems sometimes like another world away I'll never get back to and I began to wonder if a certan someone from back there wouldn't mind hearing from me if you get my drift so here I am writing to you. Well thats all for now I will write again soon its awful hot here, worse than home. Your frend Tommy.' "

Rebecca clapped again, as if the letter were a present to her.

Dad looked as if he weren't sure how he felt, pleased or mad. He was frowning and smiling all at once. "Well," he began. But then he didn't say anything else.

My letter made me a local celebrity. Tommy's parents came all the way over from Hog Island to read it, too. They had gotten one from him earlier but hadn't had another, so they wanted to see how he was doing. Rebecca began to babble about weddings and dresses and being a bridesmaid. I read the letter over several times, but I didn't see where it had even hinted at such things. After a while, though, I fell into thinking the same. I had never had a boy like me before. I hadn't ever had a beau or been admired the way Rebecca generally was. I began almost to like Tommy Kellum.

So I began to make up my reply. I wrote it, and then rewrote it—in my head. Then I couldn't decide how to sign it. "Your friend" didn't seem to fit. I had never been Tommy's friend. Was he really saying that now I was supposed to be something more?

For the next few days I went about my chores, though I couldn't say now what they were. The blood fizzed in my veins like soda water, as if I'd been picked up and shaken hard, then set back on Earth again. My family must have seen the same old Annie washing out clothes and hanging them to dry; pulling chickweed and wire grass so it wouldn't choke out the squash; cooking oyster stew and biscuits for dinner and not burning it any worse than usual. I must have done these things, for no one complained otherwise. Becca rattled on about boyfriends and wedding dresses, then went quiet and skittish when Tommy's parents came again to visit. His mother hugged me tight, tears in her eyes. His father shook my hand until I thought it would fall off. Afterward, though, Dad said little, and Mam even less.

Everyday tasks began to feel like a dream I only walked through. For that flimsy blue square had suddenly made real to me another, mysterious world; one I had never cared much about or desired to see. Yet now it held, at an unimaginable distance from Yaupon Island, a person who spent part of his days picturing me, Annie Revels. A person who was perhaps even at that moment making plans which concerned me.

Had anyone back at the Hog Island School ever told me one day I would daydream about such as this, I would have been too amazed to laugh. Tommy Kellum, familiar as a freckle on my hand, had been made strange by his long journey away from us. And I was no longer "birdy Annie," the skinny girl with a hopeless nest of tangled hair. No, I had been become A Certain Someone.

So I agonized over my reply, choosing and rejecting words and all the possible sentences I could make of them—but all in my head before I dared think of putting anything on paper. And as the days passed I began to recall good qualities I had never before noticed in all the years I had known Tommy. Perhaps he had been not so much a bully, as a leader who simply knew what he wanted, even as a child. And hadn't he once given his own apple to my little sister? Surely no one could deny that he had beautiful, large brown eyes. Would it be forward of me to mention any of these things? I decided it would. At least, in the first letter. And how should I sign it? "Sincerely" was too formal. "Fondly" sounded indecent. Mayhap the simple "Your Friend" was best after all. Even brash, loud Tommy had been too shy to go farther than that.

My head spun. I couldn't hold a pencil, or frame a complete thought. But at the end of the week Dad said he had to go over to Willis Wharf again, and I felt I could put it off no longer. So one night after everyone else was in bed I sneaked back out to the kitchen, lit the kerosene lamp, and got out my steel-nib pen and an old bottle of school ink. Then, I composed my reply.

Dear Tommy,

I did get your letter, and you were right—I was surprised. I knew you had gone to the front, but did not expect to hear from you, or that you thought of me as A Certain Someone, as you said. Your parents came to visit and I read your letter to them, I hope you don't mind. Your mother wants to know, did you receive the soap and the cake she sent.

I am sorry about your friends who died.

What is it like Over There, flat like this place, or full of

hills? Perhaps you are near a real French city. Are the roads
as wide across as our broad water? Our newspapers, which
are a bit old when we get them, say "Our Doughboys' spirit
is high." I wondered, though, if that is right, after reading
your letter. But I hope it is true.

I also wondered what you would like to hear. The news
from home I guess, though as you must recall there is not
much generally to report. But I will do my best to find things
to tell. Everyone says that soon Kaiser Bill will give up and
the war will be over. Then you will be home again and we
will all be glad. I will too.

Your Friend,
Annie

Dad needed to deliver some old anchors and cans of
drippings we'd saved up for the war effort. We rode across
in the bar cat; I kept the letter tucked in my pocket, patting
it often to make sure it hadn't blown overboard.

While Dad went off to look at new line and nets, I
walked up to the post office counter at the E. L. Willis
Store. This time Mr. Willis, instead of looking through me
the way he usually did, spoke first and even winked at me.
He told me to be sure to give his best to my brave lad
Tommy.

He was so friendly and jovial it made me nervous. "I'd
like to mail this please," I said, trying not to shuffle my
feet; trying to sound as if I mailed letters to sweethearts all

the way over in France every day. I handed over the envelope and waited while he licked a finger and thumbed slowly through the book for the postage rate. At last he found the right page. I paid for my stamp, thanked him, and turned away.

"One second there, young miss," he called out after me.

I turned, feeling awful dread. But all he said was, "Seems like I got one here for you, too." He hesitated, as if he'd like to open and read it himself, but finally held out another thin blue square.

I took the nearly weightless letter from his outstretched hand and went to sit on the bench outside the grocery, which was empty of geezers for a change. I read silently, ready to savor what would be, this time, all for me.

Dear Annie

I hope you got my last letter I know it takes a while to go across France and all that water. There has been some terribel fighting here some of my buddies are killed in such terribel bloody ways as I won't repeat. Its all a big mess of mud and blood you have never seen the like and I hope you never do. We only eat spoiled food and clean our guns and wait to see if we are going to be ded in the morning. It makes a fellow think when you have got maybe not much time left and so I worried maybe my last letter wasnt to the point. Im sure you knew of course the Someone I mentioned is your sister Rebecca but now I think I had better come to the cruks of the matter which is that I intend to ask her to marry when I get back if I do but somehow it seemed easier to write and get you to talk to her for me because she is young and you were always like one of the boys Annie and I never was afraid to fight or rassle or talk to you like a man. So I am counting on you to play cupid for yours truly

    Tommy

I don't know how long I sat there staring at the piece of paper in my hand. It seemed hard that I had just gotten a taste of what it was to be admired and noticed and made to feel special, even by someone I wasn't sure I liked, much less wanted to marry. No matter what Tommy said about me being one of the boys, I was a girl and wasn't ever going to be anything else. Certainly not a waterman; Dad had made that clear. So if I didn't marry and have a family, then what would I be and who? What would I do for the rest of my life? There were factories, I'd heard, in North Carolina, where single girls worked; I knew Jennie Floyd had gone there to spin cotton into towels and sheets.

But to sit in a big, loud room full of greasy, clattering engines all day, to never even see a glimpse of the water . . . I couldn't feature it. Some of the older women had moved away from the islands just over to the Shore, to pack seafood in crates to be shipped up north. I had seen these women around the wharf, with their heads wrapped in bandannas and their hands scarred as old gloves from oyster knives and spiny, razor-edged crab shells, their bodies thick and stiff from sitting all day, their mouths pressed thin and mean as scaling knives from cursing like men. Now I suspected that would be my fate, too.

Then I remembered. The letter, *my* letter. Tommy would get it and read I'd thought he wanted me, not Rebecca. What a fool I had made of myself. Old skinny-fanny, birdy Annie had actually believed Tommy Kellum was sweet on her. He could share that with his poor friends, to cheer them all up. What a laugh they could all have.

I stood suddenly, panic squeezing my chest. I rushed back to the post office desk in the corner of the store, Tommy's letter still clutched in my hand.

"Mr. Willis," I said, breathing hard, as if I'd run miles. "I need that letter, the one I just gave you. I need it back."

The postmaster was sorting envelopes and magazines and catalogs and sliding them into the boxes which lined one wall. Without looking up he said, "Stamped and canceled, all set to go."

"But it isn't gone, is it? And I have to have it back."

He stopped sorting, looked over and frowned at me. "Young miss, that's U.S. mail. I don't tamper with government property for anybody."

"But—"

"Now if you forgot to put in a kiss, or scratch enough Xs and Os, or some such nonsense, do it next time. What's so blasted important it won't wait?"

I stared at him, my mouth open. Nothing came to mind.

I had forgotten what a stickler for the rules, what a cantankerous old coot Mr. Willis had always been.

He smiled sourly and turned away, as if the problem was solved to everyone's satisfaction.

I leaned on the counter then, trying to look as if I might cry. "Well, may I just have it a moment to write a little postscript on the back? Please?"

He sighed, and slapped down the stack of mail he'd been sorting. He picked up my letter, which had been lying on the counter next to him all along, and slid it across to me. "Thirty seconds, mind you," he snapped.

"Oh, yes, sir. Thank you," I said as sweetly as I could muster. I set down Tommy's letter to me, then picked up mine and tore it across once, twice, three times. I stuffed the pieces in my skirt pocket. I didn't care if Mr. Willis called the sheriff; anything would be less painful than having that letter reach France.

The postmaster gaped, his face reddening. "What in the . . . what are you . . . why, I can't . . ." he sputtered, scowling at me. "Fool women." He picked up the mail again and began dealing it into the boxes savagely, like red-hot playing cards. "Damned waste of good postage."

Just then, Dad came around the corner, a new net over his shoulder. "Letter from your sweetheart again, eh," said Dad gruffly, but he looked pleased. "Well, come along then. Got to get back."

I should have told him then. I meant to, but I couldn't think how to begin. I felt angry at Rebecca, it seemed as if she had stolen something from me. Yet it was hard to decide exactly what she had done wrong. She hadn't lied, or played unfair, or charmed Tommy away. He had never been mine—and I had never truly wanted him before.

So I only nodded at Dad, folded the letter, and slipped it in my pocket before I rose to follow him to the boat.

I hid the second letter in my drawer in the bureau with the first one, telling myself I would soon explain the misunderstanding. In a day or two, I would tell Rebecca that Tommy admired her, not me. But not just yet. At dinner that night I said hardly a word, though Rebecca teased me for news of "my soldier" until Dad finally told her to mind her food and leave me be.

Mam seemed to be having a good night, and she smiled at me and patted my hand across the table. "We'll make you a nice trousseau, child, and pack it in cedar and lavender. And we'll pray for your Tommy. He'll come home safe, don't you worry none."

But of course I worried. Not so much about Tommy, I'm shamed to say, but about myself and my sudden change of status in the world. Soon Rebecca would be the one who got letters from far off and would work on making things to save up for her own home. Not me. *I shouldn't begrudge my own sister,* I thought. Yet I did. I did.

A week later, the letter still lay in my drawer beneath my underclothes. Each time I opened the drawer, I saw the edge of pale blue there accusing me. But I would slam it shut and think, *Tomorrow. Or the next day.* Until I finally understood that it was too late; I could not tell.

Fighting got hot in Europe at that time, and folks went out of their way to be kind to me. Their nice words felt like slaps sometimes. I wanted to scream when they patted my shoulder or my hand. A couple of months passed, and then Tommy's parents got a telegram.

The first I knew of it was a Saturday morning, when Mr. Kellum, Tommy's dad, appeared at our door. It was pouring rivers out, but I could see by his red-rimmed eyes that the water on his face wasn't all rain.

Before I could say a word or ask a question, he folded me in his huge arms and sobbed as if he'd never stop. So then I knew: Tommy wouldn't be coming back at all.

When Dad came out, I managed to get loose, and I rushed to my room. To hide, not to grieve, as they thought. Later, Dad told me Tommy was buried somewhere in France, where red poppies grow like chickweed. So only a memorial service would be held at the Methodist church on Hog Island. I said I didn't want to go, and everyone, even Mam, looked at me strangely.

"Never mind," I heard Dad say to them as I left the dinner table. "She's addled with grief, is all."

The funeral was a torment to us all, though for different reasons. They had saved a place for me in the front pew, next to the Kellums. I sat there with hot, dry eyes and listened to the quiet sobs of Tommy's mother. I felt the shudder of a sigh from his father, beside me, for he'd draped a consoling arm about my shoulders. I sat for what seemed like days on that rigid wooden pew, but I couldn't say exactly what the minister droned on about all that time, standing over that empty pine box. None of it stuck, perhaps because it seemed to have all to do with honor, and I suppose you could say I had none. For it occurred to me that now that Tommy was dead, there was no need to tell, ever. When this thought entered my head, I felt such a mingled rush of shame and relief that I must have reeled in my seat, for Tommy's father tightened his arm around my shoulder and asked if I felt faint. All I could do was shake my head.

The next morning before dawn, I took the letters from the bureau and went out to the beach behind the house where the family graveyard stood. I dug a hole in the sand and covered the pale blue pages up. Then I got down on my knees and begged Tommy to understand and to forgive, if he could. The wind whipped spray off the water, and I welcomed its chill needles on my bare arms. I needed some penance to do, and it was a start.

Young Sam Doughty returned the next month on crutches, missing some toes, and even quieter than before. I saw him at Willis Wharf, hobbling around, his face pale as a ghost, his body thinner, eyes stricken as a wounded rabbit's. I saw him one time, when we came to town for supplies. I watched from a distance, wondering if he'd served with Tommy, if they had huddled together in a muddy ditch and talked of home, even though Dad had told me Sam had been in Italy, not France. Before I got up my nerve to ask him anything, the war ended.

My father had been too old to go fight in Europe, and so I'd thought him safe. Not that I never worried about him; the dangers of the sea are no secret to any waterman's family, and they are always close at hand. Even young men die, get washed overboard or tangled in a net and drown. Or sometimes, like God's terrible joke, get hooked on their own gear and dragged under. My father was only fifty-six, though he looked a deal older from years of salt water and sun on his face. His forearms were a crisscross map of scars from razor-edged shells and crushing claws and wicked-sharp spines. I suppose he'd had a pretty good run. But who ever thinks of losing a parent sudden, no matter what their age?

I turned nineteen the week before the Coast Guard came to tell us about Dad. The day it happened was sunny, calm, with a light breeze out of the south. I was working the garden in an old shirt and a pair of Dad's cast-off khaki pants. I stubbornly refused to give up wearing them, and had finally convinced my father that they were more modest for certain chores around the house.

"Besides," I'd said, "who will ever see me in them but family? And it will save on dress material, Dad." Being frugal, he had found that hard to argue with.

I was weeding the rows, and Rebecca was in the house, once again washing Mam's hair in preparation for a new hairdo. Then I knew they would look at old magazines, and my sister would try to fix the two of them up in the latest styles, swan around in old stuff from the attic trunk. Or rework a castoff dress to look like some swell outfit in an ad. They never quite did, of course. As I hoed and chopped and pulled, I resolved that Rebecca would at least make lunch. And do the dishes after, as well.

When I heard the sound of a motor, I looked up and saw a launch cutting a wake toward our dock. I felt my stomach tighten, even though I didn't think, *Something's happened to Dad.* Our only guests recently had been the Kellums, the week before, to tell us they were moving south to the Outer Banks. We'd heard Mr. Kellum had gotten bad to drink in the months after they lost Tommy. But they were gone now; it wouldn't be them. I had had trouble even meeting their eyes while they were here. But I just couldn't see what good it would do to set things straight by then. It seemed only one more grief to lay upon them. But I admit, I felt as relieved as sorry when I heard they were going. Selfish, I know. But there it was.

So when I saw the boat coming, I decided it must hold folks from the mainland, after some crabs to boil or a mess of steamer clams for supper. Everyone around knew they could always count on George Revels to have the best. But rarely did anyone, even acquaintances, come all the way to the house to buy.

The tide was at low ebb, so the two men who jumped out into the water had to drag their skiff over mud and old oyster beds, then push it through the shallows up to the beach. I stopped jerking at wire grass and shaded my eyes to watch. Then I saw them screw down hats on their heads; not fishermen's caps but fancy white ones with bills. The older man's potbelly strained the cloth of his uniform jacket. I'd seen him before, buying from Dad. He was Coast Guard, in charge of the station at Cobb's Island. Dad had always referred to him as the chief.

The other one I didn't know. He was a young, birdy fellow with a wind-reddened turkey neck, who picked his way through the water as if he couldn't stand to get his blessed pants wet.

They saw me, too, but didn't wave or hail me. Instead, they looked dead somber, and I felt that chill again, stronger. The young one glanced sullenly around, as if mayhap he had someplace better to be. I waited on them a minute, the bad feeling growing worse. Then, suddenly, so quick I surprised myself, I jumped up and without even brushing the dirt from my knees turned and ran to the house. I rushed inside, panting, and shut and bolted the door.

"What's the matter?" asked Rebecca, from the kitchen. She was humming a song, some old-as-the-hills ballad about eternal love and dying soldiers. I thought sometimes she was almost sorry the war was over. To her, the idea of all those boys going out in new uniforms and getting shot

like black ducks in a marsh had seemed romantic. It was
that foolish movie stuff she read about, is all.

She had Mam at the deep, iron sink, rinsing away. She
glanced over at me. "Look like you seen the devil on a
clamshell, Annie," she said.

I didn't answer. Just twitched the faded flour-sack curtains shut on the kitchen windows. Rebecca wrapped a
towel around Mam's head, then came over and pulled the
curtains back to look.

"Get away from there," I snapped.

She looked at me in surprise. "Whatever for?"

"Because I said so."

"Well, bless me." She raised her eyebrows and looked
put out. "That's no good reason at all."

Of course there was a knock, and she reached for the
latch. I shook my head, but the damn fool opened the door
anyhow. She smiled out at the two men standing there
wringing their hats, as if they were here for tea.

"Well, come in. Come right on in," she said, fluffing her
hair, smiling like she'd invited them herself.

And in they came, dripping saltwater and beach grit over
my just-swept floor.

The chief doffed his white hat and looked at Mam, standing in the middle of the room in her towel turban. "Beg
your pardon, Missus Revels. There's been an accident."

Mam blinked at him and cocked her head sidewise, like
a finch. I was pretty sure she wasn't really taking his words

in. This hadn't been one of her good days; she'd stayed awake with a migraine all the night before.

He cleared his throat. "George, he is your husband?"

She nodded. "My George, he's a good man," she said.

The chief looked stricken and shuffled his feet. "Well, ma'am, seems he was out past Cobb's Island, pulling pots this morning. A boatload from Cobb's saw him bend to reach for something, then just fall over the side. They motored up real quick, but he'd already gone like a stone. We've looked up and down the shore and all around the island. No sign of him. I do hate to tell bad news, Missus Revels, but—"

Surely he could see Mam wasn't listening. She was looking away from him, at my sister. "Who is this gentleman, Becca? Did you offer a cup of coffee?"

"No, Mam," said Rebecca. She looked from them to our mother. I could see at least she understood something was bad wrong. She made a move as if to go to the kitchen, but I put out a hand and stopped her.

"Bossy," she hissed at me, but low, under her breath. She folded her arms, but she looked more worried than peeved.

The men turned to me, both at once, as if my high-handedness had told what they needed to know of who was in charge.

"My sympathies to you and the family, Miss Revels," said the chief. He spoke rapidly, in the flat, clipped tones of a Yankee come-here. The sound of his words fell on me like sharp-edged rain, hurtful and unreal. "Your father was a fine man. We got his boat tied up now at the station. Do you want—I mean, should we bring it over for you?"

I couldn't take in all they were saying, either. Yet I had to. I knew what the words meant, anyway. Dad was dead. Drowned.

"Yes," I said. "Bring it."

I felt angry beyond reason at the two men who carried the news, as if they'd had a hand in his death. Nonsense of course, but I couldn't stop myself. I gritted my teeth and tried hard to sound calm and grown up, but I could only just force myself to be polite.

The younger one was staring. I didn't like the sneaky way he eyed Rebecca when the chief wasn't looking his way. That day my sister wore a thin, print summer dress, damp with heat and water from the sink, and not much under it. I noticed his peach-fuzz cheeks had blotched all red. The apple of his throat bobbed up and down twice, hard.

Most of the time I forgot Rebecca was beautiful. By nineteen, I still hadn't grown out of the gawky stage and was far away from good looks myself. I had eyes and a good mirror, but never saw much difference day to day. My hair had long since grown back from the ragged boy's cut I gave myself at thirteen, but I never thought on how I looked or what I wore, as long as it was comfortable and covered the important parts. On the rare occasions we went over to the mainland, it was like when we were kids again. Old ladies and shop clerks cooed over my sister's hair, her soft, pale skin. Young men and old stared on the street. Like the children at school, they all took notice.

Of course, I was supposed to be dead Tommy's girl. Broken up and pining for a brave soldier who would never come home.

And besides, Dad had always had a reputation for being a loner, a bit of a hard man. I knew he'd seen a brawl or two in his younger days. When he scowled at those staring boys, they paled and scooted off. I guess the older men had been in enough fights with him, growing up, to know better than to try and rob a Revels's cradle. Or insult an almost-widow.

But Dad wasn't here now. He wouldn't be coming home at all.

If I'm to be the one in charge, so be it, I thought. I moved forward, ushering the two men, hats still in hand, to the door. I flapped and shooed them on, the way you would yard chickens. Once they crossed the threshold, I slammed the door and latched it fast.

I turned back to my sister and mother, to say something. My mouth opened and closed silently. I must have looked like a hooked fish; I recall I felt that helpless.

Finally I managed, "You heard them, Becca. Mam. Dad's gone."

They looked at me silently. My mother seemed calm, but my little sister's face was shocked and white, her eyes round as cork fishing floats. The both of them seemed like oversized children I had suddenly birthed, innocent beyond reason and without a clue. Teary-eyed, her bottom lip trembling, Rebecca somehow managed to look even prettier. She shook her head. Her hands trembled, too, and crept up to play with Mam's damp hair, moving like small, smooth, white animals, burrowing through the long, black silk of it for comfort.

Worst of all was that my mother appeared shrunken to me all of a sudden, like the shriveled, mummified corpse that had once washed up after a storm, floated all the way to us from some cemetery or sunken boat after a hurricane. Mam's ears were good; I knew she had heard what the chief said. But had she understood a lick?

I felt all of a sudden orphaned. That even though Mam had been this way for years, I had lost two parents at once.

"Mam," I said, picking up the dish towel Rebecca had dropped on the floor. Twisting it in my hands until I thought I heard it tear. I didn't want to be the one in charge anymore. Not of this. I wanted someone to hug me and pat my shoulder and tell me it would be all right soon. "Mam," I repeated. "About Dad. What shall we do now?"

Some thoughts were already crossing my mind. Mayhap she'd want to have more of a search for his body. Or decide what to do if it wasn't found, such as put up a cross, later.

She looked at me and shook her head. "Why, wait till your father comes in, Annie," she said. "He'll take care. Now, you'd best hop to get dinner going. He likes it on the table at five sharp."

*   *   *

That night, Rebecca got on me about the funeral we ought to have, even if the coffin was empty. She wanted to order a fancy casket from the mainland. She wanted a regular funeral with flowers and new black dresses.

"Annie, you want folks to think we're chinchy? Our own dad," she whined.

I soon set her straight. Dad would have been aghast; he'd have thought that a terrible waste. Most of the time, we had plenty to eat and good clothes to wear, but a fancy brass-fitted casket was a thing he'd never have approved. Rebecca knew that as well as I did. She'd been disappointed often enough in a sudden fancy she'd gotten for some kind or other of pricey store goods. I have to admit she usually took the disappointment well. It was just that every now and then, she'd get her hands on a magazine. She wanted to be a woman in her tastes, but to me she was still a squit, a mama's girl putting on airs.

She liked to stick close to Mam even now, and as our mother's health and mind seemed to worsen, the two might have switched places. I think my sister tried to be the mama. She didn't dare to tell me how to dress and fix my hair; she knew I'd put a stop to that right quick. Fine with me to let Mam be her big live doll, to dress and fix up. Or her child, even. I never wanted any part of those games. Though sometimes, when I saw them huddled on the couch or sitting at the table, Rebecca laughing and turning pages, I felt a dull ache in my stomach, a hollow-ness there. But I didn't want to be sitting next to them, I'm sure of that. I just told myself they were both lazy and mindless as house cats, that I wasn't missing a thing.

So I was surprised when, after I squashed her grand funeral plans, my sister blew her nose and said, as if it had already been discussed and decided, "I'll pick out the hymns." She went to the shelf and took down the Methodist hymnal from next to the family Bible.

"All right," I said, feeling a slight lessening of the throb in my head. I had to keep reminding myself. Dad was gone. Dad was dead.

And Mam was getting more and more childish in her mind. But at least, I thought, my little sister might be counted on to grow up yet. I recalled her white face earlier on, her expression so like the stricken look she'd given me all those years ago when for spite I'd pushed her away from Granny Jester's bed. I felt ashamed all over again and bent to give her a quick hug.

She looked startled, then squeezed my hand. "Poor Annie," she said. "I know he loved you the best. That must be hard."

I felt the held-back tears start to my eyes then and had to turn and go out the door and back to the garden, where I yanked savagely at the wild onion and wire grass for a long time before I could come inside again.

*   *   *

They brought Dad home the next morning. He'd washed ashore at Cobb's Island on the high tide. The Cobbs, or whoever among them discovered the body, must have recognized him. Still, I wondered that they had called the government rather than bring him along themselves like family, or at least neighbors. Two solemn guardsmen followed me inside. They laid him out where I pointed, on the kitchen table. It was the only place I could think to put him except one of our own beds, and that seemed too grim.

But this was just Dad, I reminded myself. He had drowned as watermen sometimes did, working at what he loved best. He hadn't taken sick, and then mad, and shouted and cursed and turned purple and thrown dishes like Granny Jester. He wouldn't be a ghost come back to frighten his own kin.

The Coast Guard men stepped back from the table, then straightened their dark wool uniforms, brass buttons winking in the dim inside light. They waited, quiet and respectful. I took a deep breath and turned to look at last on the dead body of my father, whom I'd never speak to again. Who'd not speak to me, either. And yes, that was hard, hard.

But still it wasn't as bad as I had feared.

My sister came in the kitchen, took one look at the body, at the runnels of water, little streams trailing off the wooden table from his still-sodden clothes. She made a pitiful sound in her throat, like a trapped mouse, and fled to the bedroom where Mam lay sleeping.

"Rebecca," I called, wanting some family next to me just then. I heard sobbing and sniffling from the back, but she wouldn't come out. After a moment, I thanked the men.

"You want us to call someone? For help with the laying out," said the chief. He spoke right to me still, as if it was understood I headed the house, not even asking anymore for Mam. "And then—were you wanting it to be at sea?"

"Wanting what?" That made no sense to me at all.

"The burial. Some of the watermen I've talked to, they thought . . ."

He looked embarrassed, and turned his hat around in his hands.

I hesitated, then shook my head. Wouldn't look right at him, because I knew that in fact Dad would probably like best to be put into the sea, to follow the water forever. He'd told me more than once he'd rather be out there at daybreak than eat or drink. But it seemed like all we had left now, for the family, was this body. I couldn't bring myself to let go of it.

"No," I said. "Thank you, but no."

Still they hesitated. So did I. I tried hard but couldn't think of anyone to call. We had always been Methodists through and through. But after Mam got so ill, months passed sometimes before we got to services at the Hog Island church. The older ladies who all knew her had mostly passed on or were unsteady themselves. Though this had never bothered me before, it seemed shameful we couldn't muster a pack of grieving relatives or friends, or at least anticipate a flock of church biddies carting baked goods and lace hankies.

"No," I repeated. "We can manage."

I did accept their offer to dig the grave for us, though I was strong enough and the ground soft so that I could have easily done it myself. We decided to put my father in a sandy spot on the sea side of the island, near where Granny Jester had been laid to rest, if that was the right word. Dad would lie between her and our long-dead baby brother.

There at least he could have a view of the sea for eternity.

The two men borrowed a spade and set off, and I went to find a clean sheet for a shroud.

Then I turned back to Dad.

He looked pale and slightly bloated. Smelled strong of seawater and fish, but certainly that was nothing new. The hardest thing was that his skin felt cold and rubbery beneath my fingers, but I set my teeth and squinted so I wouldn't have to look straight on at my father, who'd been killed by the water it seemed he sometimes loved more than us.

I dragged and hauled at his clothes, but for the longest time couldn't get them off. The sodden cloth clung tight as barnacles to his dead skin. So I went and got the kitchen shears out of the drawer and cut them off in strips. I filled a bowl with hot water and took a clean rag and a bar of soap and began washing the salt and bits of seaweed off him. His dead eyes, still open to slits, seemed to regard me doing all this, but didn't appear to pass judgment on the job I was making of it.

I hesitated when I got to his underdrawers. I had once or twice glimpsed my father naked after he got in from a long day out on the water. Mam had always insisted, back when her mind was still strong enough to be house-proud, that Dad must wash the fish stink off before he came inside. So he'd strip bare behind a wooden partition outside the kitchen door and pour two pails of salt water, then a pail of fresh from the well pump, right over his head. When I was grown big enough, I was expected to haul the water and once, when he was staggering tired, he had lurched forward to take the pail from me. I had seen his man's thing then, swinging between his legs, a wrinkled and reddened tube of flesh that looked useless and pitiful to me.

I did not want to look at it now. So I had to scold myself: Would I rather the crabs had gotten to him, and nibbled off parts to make it easy on me? Finally I took a deep breath and yanked at his drawers. Unlike his outer clothes, they peeled off quick, but with a cold, wet sound that made me shiver. I set about blindly sponging him off there with another clean rag.

As I did, I cursed my mother under my breath, though it was not her fault she was old and half loony. But in truth, this laying out was her job, and here her daughter was doing it all alone while she sat in the other room, in some world far removed from dead bodies and responsibilities and burying.

Then I stopped scrubbing, the wet rag dripping in my hand. Now that my father was gone from us, who would do his work? How would we eat? Who'd be both parent and provider, father and mother? I was not yet twenty. I had never even kissed a man, or gone to sea, or given birth to a child. I had for consolation only a sham romance with a boy who had never really wanted me. It seemed at that moment that not only had I not done a thing I wanted to yet, now I had no prayer of a chance for it in the future. What was left of my family was bound to hang around my neck like chain on a sheet anchor.

I had loved my father, and perhaps he'd loved me, but he'd never said so. I had only wanted to be like him, but he would not allow it. A crippled family and two old oyster work boats, the bar cat and the bateau, that's all in the world Dad had left me.

I felt bitterness welling up in my chest then, and I did cry. Hot tears dripped onto my father's still body as I scrubbed and scrubbed again. They stuck here and there to the mat of curled gray hair that covered his chest, useless as rain on dead summer grass.

Five

I learned pretty fast how to operate the old, eight-foot oyster tongs, though it was wicked hard on my arms and shoulders. I knew some already about placing crab traps, from those days when I was small and Dad had taken me out. Sometimes he'd let me heave the pots overboard. In those days, I had liked to turn and look over my shoulder from my seat in the bow and watch the floats bobbing behind us. I thought they were a trail home, like the bread crumbs in the fairytale, only safer. Even the greediest seagull wouldn't try to gobble up a cork fishing float. The bobbing red and white markers, spinning and tilting in the current like a child's top, would always be there to show us the way home to Yaupon Island.

But these same bright floats, marked with Dad's colors, became a torment to me. All day, after I had sailed out in

the flat-bottomed skiff or rowed when the wind was dead
calm, I spent heaving the wire-mesh traps out over the side,
then, later, pulling them up again. Too late I understood
that all those years ago he had taken their weight and num-
bers himself, only pretending I was helping him lift one or
two.

Soon I also understood, although I had learned in school
that the proper term was *dredge,* why all watermen both
bayside and seaside called them drudge boats. For that's
what oystering was: a drudgery. My back ached long before
it was time to come in. My hands sprouted splinters and
cuts and blisters that rose and swelled and burst, leaking
water until Dad's old canvas gloves were glued to my
smarting palms. I was already tanned and wore a hat in the
afternoons. But the sun reflected off the water all day so
bright, I burned red even when it was overcast. The skin
on my face and neck felt tight and drawn, and I was sure
it was slowly turning to leather. Soon I'd be seamed as an
old wallet, creased as the taciturn codgers who chewed and
spat as they sat on the liar's bench at the E. L. Willis Store.
The ones who had said—at least when I was little and still
had the potential of late-blooming looks ahead of me—
what a young lady I was getting to be. A glance in the hall
mirror told me they wouldn't say so now.

So I started wearing Dad's old clothes, his long-sleeved
shirts, his heavy wool and cotton pants. And then, except
for my hands and cheeks, I didn't burn. I sweated instead.
The smell of cut fish bait and rotten chicken necks mixed

with my own salt-and-pepper smell of woman sweat, until at the end of the day I could hardly stand myself. I would strip off my stinking clothes, as Dad had used to do, before I came in the house. Then it was Rebecca's turn to bring the buckets of water I poured over my head—first salt, then fresh—until I felt less fish and more human again.

Those bright markers haunted me at night, too, while I slept. In my dreams they slipped their lines and floated off so that I could come back and circle round and round until I was an old woman like Mam, and never find the traps below that held crabs I needed to sell to keep us all alive and fed and clothed. They streamed off in the wake of my dreams, cheerful red stripes rising up on swells and then disappearing down in the troughs, out of sight, towed by the Gulf Stream away to another country, where children splashed and played with my candy-striped markers in a gentle surf, imagining them to be naught but pretty toys.

I'd wake from these nightmares sweating, panting in fear, wanting in the darkness to go jump in the tiny battered bar cat and go check on the plaguey traps, though it was still night and I couldn't see my hands before me.

The day we'd buried Dad, I'd turned from his narrow, sandy grave, and Rebecca had slipped her soft, white hand into my bigger, sun-browned one. She'd squeezed it tight.

"We're all that's left, Annie. We have to take care of Mam now. Dad would have wanted it so."

"Yes," I'd said quickly and squeezed back. I felt a tightness in my chest, and thought grief for Dad and the gripping love I felt just then for my sister had pushed the breath right out. But under my breastbone I also felt a gnawing pain, as if a small animal was eating right into my heart, his dark weight making it difficult to breathe.

Sure, I'd wanted to go out on the water, to work the boat. But I had wanted to go out with my father. I never dreamed of taking Dad's place as head of the family. I was frightened all of a sudden and wanted to fling her little cool-fingered hand away. Now it felt damp nestled in my palm, like some disgusting white thing dug up by mistake in the garden.

Instead, I made myself hold on all the way back to the house. And Rebecca smiled up at me, trusting her big sister as she had when we were kids and her head reached no higher than my belly button.

I'd always thought I would stay here forever, tied to this place. It hadn't occurred to me before that I would be tied forever to them, too. To Mam and Rebecca.

I did like wearing Dad's clothes out on the water, though. Soon I wore them all the time. For a while they still smelled of him: tobacco and the clothes soap and a faint whiff of whiskey. Finally, the smell faded, as the clothes took on my shape, trousers bunched up thinner in the middle, shirt billowing over my waist, tighter over my slight swell of woman's hips.

Then one afternoon, about a month or so after the funeral, as I slumped in the bottom of the boat catching my breath, I realized I couldn't detect a hint of Dad's smell on his old shirt at all. He was no longer with me. For a blind moment, it was as if he'd died all over again. I wiped tears off my face, smearing my cheeks with fish scales and bilge slime. Maybe my father had kept me ashore because he only wanted to spare me all this hard, stinking work. Maybe that was why he'd beat me for trying so hard to turn myself into a boy. Maybe he had, after all, loved me best. But not enough to say so.

At home, Rebecca was hopeless in the garden. All she wanted to grow was marigolds. She left the radishes in the ground till they were tough and bitter, the lettuce went unpicked so long it blew to seed, and beetles ate the collard greens because it made her shudder to pick off bugs with her bare fingers. So I'd send her to the other side of the island with Mam, holding hands, to gather wild plums and beach cherries, and blackberries in summer. Then I'd stretch out on my belly in the dirt, between the furrows after a long day on the water, lifting my aching arms only far enough to pinch out whatever crafty bugs hid in the folds of the leaves, waiting to chew our precious food to tatters.

One night I fell asleep out there in the dirt and didn't even hear Rebecca calling me in from the doorway. Somehow, she never thought to look in the garden or else was afraid to come out, so I woke at dawn stiff as leather left in the rain, riddled and pocked with mosquito bites, aching and sticky with dew. I opened a tired, gluey eye to see one of our skinny hogs nosing at my feet, ready to eat me, no doubt, if I hadn't sat up and shouted him away.

I looked up, surprised not to see buzzards circling, too. If they had been coasting there, I might have dropped back down and happily made them a meal, just to escape my aches and pains. Instead, I got up and went out again without even changing my stiff, salt-and-fish-scale-crusted clothes. That morning, I only took time to splash water on my face, drink a cup of cold coffee, and bolt down a gagging hunk of Rebecca's tough, dry molasses bread. Then I stuffed a cold baked sweet potato in my pocket for lunch and headed out, dirty and cramped and miserable.

Of course it would be that day I met Nathan Combs.

By noon, I was tired to death and smelled so bad I wished I'd let the hog eat me. The day was hotter than usual, even for July. I decided to anchor the bateau off Steamer Island, a deserted marshy moon-shaped spit of land with a deep tidal pond screened by reeds and spartina grass. I lowered the sail, then stripped off my clothes and stretched full length in the water, spread-eagled in the sun, letting the heat loosen my tight muscles. I didn't care if I burned from titties to toes; it felt good to wash off the sludge and grime of the day before.

I glanced down at my stomach, pale white and wavery-looking under the water, my breasts, too, bright against the brown of my forearms and the V of brown on my chest where the sun had tanned my skin through the open neck of Dad's green flannel shirt. My nipples were rosy pink, and the shock of cool water made them pucker and harden. I slid a hand over the rise of my pale belly and rested it on the dark tangle below.

Some nights, when I was not too tired, I did the same thing, lying on my stomach under the covers, face pressed into my pillow to muffle the moans when my slippery fingers finally stopped moving. I didn't want to wake Rebecca, who slept always without a sound, wearing an old white nightgown of Mam's, lying on her back quiet as the doll she still took to bed with her.

They felt different in the water, my hands, tanned and roughened as any waterman's. I could imagine they stroked my wet body as if they belonged to an admiring stranger. Once, I started up, thinking I'd heard a splash, the dip of an oar. Once even the dry clatter of a motor. But the sound seemed so far off, I didn't even raise my head or open my eyes.

I hated to put on the same filthy clothes after, but there was nothing else. I did feel better, even with a rime of salt drying sticky on my skin. I had forgotten for a little while that I was gangly Annie Revels, with hands and feet big as a teenage boy's, a tall clumsy woman with sun-baked skin and osprey-nest hair who had to mind the traps and trotlines and tongs and scrapers because she had no father now, nor a husband to do it, and probably never would.

I left my shirt untucked and two buttons undone so I

felt a bit cooler. I waded back out to the boat, which was pulling at the anchor as the tide ran. Off to the left was a dark smudge; thunderheads from the look of them. Squalls could come up fast on the Atlantic or cross the Eastern Shore peninsula from the bay and be just as quick gone. Nor'easters, too. I didn't like to be caught in a storm, because then the boat pitched and tossed so much I felt sick to my stomach. And because it meant a few crab-pot markers might really break free and float off, so I'd have to check them all again just to make sure. A bad storm meant silty slur would be stirred up and settle into the oyster beds. Then sometimes they died out. And I also hated storms because although I was nineteen coming up on twenty years, I was still mortally afraid of lightning.

I put back out into the channel and decided to head for home. Easy enough to check pots on the way. I decided I wouldn't tong for oysters today after all. Maybe I'd weed the garden and make a pot of greens with ham scraps, so we wouldn't have to eat Rebecca's tough, overbaked bread and leftover leathery fried pork chops. Or maybe I'd even hustle around and cook peas and dumplings, the way Mam used to make them when I was little.

We hadn't eaten that in a long time. I'd seen her fix them often enough when I was little, though. She'd shell the peas sitting out on the back porch, and when I was old enough, she had me alongside her, popping the crisp green pods and firing peas like green bullets into the pan. Rebecca was first too young to cook, then too impatient to ever make a good job of it. Even shelling peas, she managed to mangle most of her lot and we'd end up feeding the waste to the hogs.

But Mam had always made the best dumplings, from just flour and water and salt and a knob of butter. My stomach growled at the thought of a steaming bowl of green peas and dumplings floating in broth. I brailed in the sail, wanting to hurry home now. The seam of my britches, which I had yanked up high to belt above my waist, chafed between my legs. I tried to ignore it, but after a while I gave in to the tingling feeling between soreness and pleasure the press of tight material created. As I worked, I imagined a man, dark-haired, big-shouldered, leaning over me. It seemed I was naked and so was he, and down between us, where his thighs pressed on mine, a hardness slowly but insistently forced my legs apart. And when I finally gave up, gave in, he laughed—not in meanness but in delight. Then he took hold of my arms and pulled me down.

Just as I closed my eyes, nearly convinced the dream man was really there in the boat with me, an awful jolt knocked me hard to the deck. I slammed my head on the tiller on the way down, clawing at the gear and lines. The boat's timbers creaked and groaned, then she listed to the side. I finally understood through pain like a spike in my head that we had run aground on a sand shoal I'd have sworn hadn't been there that morning.

I stood again on shaky legs. Looked things over and saw I'd have to push her off, somehow, though the bateau was heavy as a barge and seemed stuck fast now. High tide already, so I couldn't wait for the rising to float me off. The keel would only take the ground that much harder if I delayed.

I jumped out. The water was only to my knees, and my boots slipped and slid in sandy muck as I scrambled across a dead oyster bed. I shoved hard as I could, and nothing happened. Shoved again, and the bateau rocked a little, as if rolling in laughter at all my useless grunting and cursing. She was definitely settling in, and I was pouring sweat despite the cool water. My gloves were in the boat and my palms bleeding again, this time from barnacle cuts. I also felt a warm trickle threading over one eyebrow from a gash I must have gotten in the fall.

"Damn it all to hell," I snarled. And then, over my grunts and gasps, I heard a faint low grumble, the water-muffled popping of a motor.

I ducked behind the side of the boat. The other watermen hadn't spoken much since I'd started working out here, nor had I said much to them. Perhaps this day I'd see someone I knew, Sam Doughty or Billy Bagwell, not one of the crusty older men who usually passed me by, faces averted, eyes blank, as though I were a heat mirage on the water. I suppose I wasn't a sight they liked: a young woman doing the kind of work most folks deemed fit only for men. The younger watermen were at least courteous at a distance and mostly left me alone, but I knew the ones my father's age and older still believed that a woman on the water meant bad luck. I could hear the rumble of Dad's voice again, saying, "Black gum against thunder," whenever I crossed paths with one of the oldsters out on the water.

Well, I had news for them all: It was a lie. I made a pretty good jag some days, and I kept my own tally. Not much got by me. "One arster is as dear as five bushels," my father used to say, and I took his words to heart. He had been neither popular nor unpopular, far as I knew. We just kept ourselves to ourselves. When he died, no one had volunteered to take up his nets or marry his daughters, so here I was, and damn them, too, if they didn't like it.

Oh, a few locals, mostly folks from church, had stopped by the house, some bringing a layer cake or a casserole or round of cornbread. But Dad was a loner, and Mam had had no fast friends left I knew of, not living alone on our island.

Well, popular or not, I had to get off the bar. So I shoved sweat-tangled hair out of my eyes, wadded it in a rough bun, jammed it all back under Dad's old hat, and stood again. Nothing I could do about the dirt on my clothes or the slime and caked mud. But then why should a waterman care about such as that?

I heard a faint sound again, like a motor, and squinted west into the sun. I saw that a small, blue-painted skiff was headed my way, rounding the marsh grass surrounding Steamer Island. A lone man stood at the tiller. He waved in my direction. As he got closer, he called out something, maybe just hailed me. I stood and waited, feeling dirty and foolish. Feeling ashamed. No waterman likes to beg for help.

Well, perhaps he would offer it before I had to ask.

The man cut the motor and drifted alongside, catching the stern of the bateau to steady the rocking of his flat-bottomed skiff. He snatched off his billed cap and grinned at me. I didn't think much of that grin. He was no water-man by his clothes, yet he looked me up and down as if he knew me well, too well. I was sure I'd never in my life set eyes on him.

"Need a hand?" he said, bracing his legs as the lapping waves of his wake rocked both our boats. He scanned my empty hold and seemed surprised. "When I saw you t'other day, she was loaded down far as she could swim. Looked like you'd caught the bottom and didn't put it back."

I nodded, shrugged. And then my damn hat blew off. My wild snarly hair whipped in the wind, first blinding me, then nearly choking me when I opened my mouth to an-swer. I watched for a look of surprise to cross his face, but if it did, he hid it quick. I had figured he would assume, from a distance, that I was a man.

If he was the least bit surprised, he recovered fast. "Ma'am," he said. "You look tuckered. Let me help you get off this bar." He had the long-voweled accent of a local, so he wasn't a come-here. Maybe a Marylandman. But I still didn't know him a lick, and wasn't about to trust a stranger, a man who wouldn't even think to offer up a name first.

He hesitated, as if waiting for me to give a signal of some sort.

"You sound like a Shoreman," I said finally. "Are you from up the county?"

He rubbed his face and laughed a little. "Excuse my bad manners. My name's Combs. Nathan Combs. I've been away a good long while. Now I work off yonder island, for the Cobb brothers."

I nodded. I'd always known the Cobbs' place was such a going affair they hired local men and even some Marylandmen to help the grown sons guide tourists out to fish or shoot. This Combs fellow could be from a ways off, the Western Shore or from over the line in Maryland. I couldn't expect to know every soul that ventured out on the water.

"I know the place," I said and shrugged again, not wanting to sound desperate. I supposed we could just run out the anchor line and get her off, but I decided to wait. I was interested to see what he'd do.

"Suppose I'd appreciate a hand," I said, as if it didn't really matter to me.

He braced himself on the gunwale and vaulted over the side, so graceful he barely made a splash in the water. He waded over, and then did a thing that nearly stopped my heart. He stood thigh deep in the water, unbuttoned his clean shirt, and stripped down to his undershirt. He dipped his good white shirt in the water. Then raised the dripping cloth, tilted my chin with a finger, and gently sponged my face.

"You're bleeding bad here, and here," was all he said, but I felt the heat creeping up my neck to my face. I'd forgotten my bruised forehead and thought for a minute he'd meant something else, since my time of the month was near. He stood so close I could smell man sweat and smoke and maybe a hint of whiskey on his breath. Except for the faint tang of some sort of spicy soap, he was much like Dad's smell. Only, to be honest, cleaner. The scent of a young man who wasn't a stranger to bathing, like some men thereabouts.

So I stood as still as I could in the current, and it never once entered my mind to flinch or pull away, even though the cut on my forehead hurt like holy bejesus as he dabbed at it.

Then he put that shirt stained with my blood back on, splotched pink in places with it, and laid his shoulder to the stern. I came out of my trance then and helped shove until we rocked her free. He boosted me up, and I climbed in again.

"You look like a woman who can manage. But would you want me to follow you in?"

I didn't know what I wanted exactly at that point, so I shook my head and gripped the tiller again.

He hauled himself back over the side, into his skiff. Then said, "Be seeing you." He grinned again, and I didn't take it amiss this time. He'd already come about and was headed back where he'd been going before I thought to call my thanks after him. I was sure he wouldn't hear me over the noise from his motor, but then he surprised me and lifted a hand to wave without looking around.

I made it back but forgot all about the peas and dumplings until it was almost dark. So I had to go out and pick them by lantern light, as the bugs nearly ate me up. I scratched mosquito bites furiously half the night and couldn't sleep the other half. Until I huddled under the covers, my face pressed to the sweat-damped cotton of my pillow. And feeling far away from my sister, who slept noiselessly as a child, I rode the hard pressure of my own hand till I was seized again with that sudden burst of hot pleasure in the dark.

Six

I began to notice Nathan Combs everywhere. Most often I was mistaken, though. For when I came abreast of an oyster dredge, I'd see that the man who turned to wave without a word, the one I'd taken at a hopeful distance to be Combs, was some potbellied geezer with few teeth left in his tobacco-stained beard or a teenage boy with red-cratered cheeks. Those times I'd feel an awful despair all out of proportion to such a simple disappointment.

One day, as I was hauling in my twelfth empty pot, my salt-crusted face slick with sweat, from around a stand of driftwood and spartina chugged one of the Cobb's fishing boats, a long low launch with a striped awning. Under it sat three hunters. They looked overdressed to me in slouch hats and city tweeds. Nathan stood in the stern at the wheel. I straightened to see him better, then remembered how I looked.

Oh Lord, I thought. Why must it be today?

I wore a pair of Dad's old khaki trousers that had long ago split; I'd whipstitched the crotch seam with marline. The pants were so loose that, even belted, they rode down to the cheeks of my behind every time I bent over. Well, too late to change into a party dress. So I jerked the waistband up and tried to pretend I didn't give a damn.

The skiff putt-putted by, bristling with expensive-looking shotguns, the tourist sportsmen gawking at my wild hair and smudged face. But as they chugged past, Nathan surprised me. He looked right at me and winked. That single twitch of his eyelid seemed to tell me we were in it together against all the overdressed, scrubbed, staring come-heres in the world. And then I surprised myself. Before I even realized I was going to do it, I raised one dirty hand, its bitten nails outlined with black grease crescents, and waved.

I thought I saw him a few more times, but always from a distance. Until one afternoon, as I was getting ready to call it a day, it was for sure that same blue skiff headed my way again. Nathan hailed me and pulled up a few feet away, then just sat for a moment. He wasn't smiling this time; instead he pointed to a wicker hamper between the seats.

"Some doctors from Annapolis got seasick," he said. "Had to take them back to Cobb. Now I have all this fancy lunch they didn't eat."

He sat quiet then, once again acting as if he'd asked a question and was waiting for my answer. I ducked my head and nodded. I wanted to think of something clever to toss back, but nothing came to me. I wasn't about to say anything too forward, anyhow. I didn't know him well enough.

He laughed, but it wasn't a mean sound. "Guess when it's been a while since you've asked a girl out, you forget exactly what to say. Would you care to have lunch with me today, Miss Annie Revels?"

I hesitated, then nodded again, still keeping my head down so he wouldn't see the smile wanting to stretch my face all silly. He came alongside and snagged the gunwale with a boat hook. He didn't have to ask or direct me. I set my anchor fast, stepped over onto the varnished plank bench across from him, and sat. Then we sped off, the one-lunger gas engine popping in my ears, in the direction of Steamer Island.

It didn't occur to me until we got there and he was handing the basket out of the boat to me that I hadn't ever actually told him my name. The notion that he'd been interested enough to go and ask someone sent a thrill to my stomach.

Nathan spread a checked cloth under the shade of a tall dune that had been wind-carved concave inside the crescent-shaped beach. I washed my hands in the tidal pool and tried not to think about the last time I'd been there, so dirty I couldn't resist stripping off all my clothes and floating belly naked to the sky just a few yards away. We sat in the shade, eating a tourist lunch of little bitty ham biscuits and fancy-swirled deviled eggs and tart green apples washed down with tea so sweet it made my teeth ache.

Last of all, he handed me a slice of chocolate pound cake, dense and buttery, dusted with a thick coat of fine-ground cocoa. I was too full already but somehow ate every crumb. I didn't even mind him watching me, though I wished I smelled of something nicer than crab shells and oyster muck. I was glad I had at least taken a bath and washed my hair the night before.

A few loose strands blew into my mouth as I opened it to take in the last bite. He reached out and tucked my hair back behind my ear. Then he took that bit of cake from my hand and tossed it into the water. He scooted across the picnic oilcloth and laid his hands on my shoulders. He leaned in close, and in a way I understood what he planned to do next. I'd seen enough of the pictures of silent film stars all wrapped around each other in Rebecca's movie magazines.

I thought I was supposed to shut my eyes at this point, so he could sweep me into his arms and dramatically bend me over backward. But I had waited pretty near twenty years to be kissed, and didn't intend to miss a thing, so I kept them wide open.

His lips were firm, still coated with cocoa from the cake, so smooth and good-tasting I wanted to lick them. But maybe that wasn't the right thing to do, so I waited to see what was. I was surprised when, the next minute, he shoved his tongue into my mouth. It pushed against mine, hot and muscular-feeling, and I was afraid for a minute I might gag on its strangeness there. But before that could happen, he eased me down on the cloth next to him, and I forgot about the foreign feel of part of him in my mouth. The tip of his tongue kept probing, exploring the hard ridges of my teeth and the soft inside of my cheek.

So this is what it's like, I thought, not really wanting to think too far ahead to what all *it* might mean, what might come next. Mam had never explained such things to me; when we were little, Dad had always turned red as a boiled crab every time Rebecca or I asked where the baby hogs had come from, or how the kittens got into the cat's belly in the first place. Finally, we had to give up asking and settle for our own shared notions, right or wrong. The details of how we ourselves had arrived had only been a deeper mystery, and certainly no one had encouraged us to look into it.

Then Nathan stopped kissing my mouth and rolled on top of me, and I forgot about baby hogs and newborn kittens. He raised up on his elbows, looked down at my face, and kissed the tip of my nose, dirty as it was. Then he licked it, the way a friendly dog might, and we both laughed.

"I better let you go home now," he said. His voice sounded different now, rougher, hoarse, next to a whisper.

"But I don't want to," I said. It was true. I wanted to lie

there in the sand and stare at him a while. And what I wanted most was for him to kiss me again.

After I said that, it seemed his expression changed. He stopped smiling and looked serious again, as solemn as he had when we'd met in the boats. He leaned on his elbows and pressed down a little harder. The warm weight of him pushed me deeper into the sand.

"Is that right," he whispered in my ear, but not like it was any kind of question.

Now I wasn't sure what to answer. So I just nodded and closed my eyes, afraid I would ruin everything if I said the wrong word. My whole body felt taut as a snagged line. I didn't think I could stand it if he suddenly stood up and took me back to my boat.

Still, the next thing that happened shocked me a good deal more than a tongue in my mouth. What he did was, he took hold of the waistband of my trousers and jerked. He did it two or three times until the rope let loose and then suddenly he had my britches down and bunched round my knees, then pushed to my ankles. I gasped, truly mortified. I had no underwear on because it had rained the last few days and Rebecca had used that as an excuse to not do any laundry while I was out. So all my underdrawers were dirty, stuffed in the clothes basket in the kitchen.

I opened my mouth to say, *No. Stop.*

But he covered my lips with his, breathing into me until I thought I might be happy to let my own breath stop and allow him do it for me from then on. I felt his hand fumbling around again, sliding between our bellies, groping for something. The rest was so fast, it's hard to recall. I was so nervous I thought to scream, not from fear but from the not knowing of what would happen next. But I didn't. I twisted to the right, meaning to sit, to get up so I could fasten my trousers again. When I squirmed under him, trying to slide away like that, he grunted something like, "Okay." Or maybe, "This way," I don't know.

"What?" I whispered.

"Never mind. I know something you'll like," he muttered in my ear.

Before I could much wonder what he might mean by that, he gently rolled me over onto my stomach and used his knees to force my legs apart. He lay on me at first, his weight heavy and warm on my back, and yet it felt so nice I didn't care that it was hard to breathe. He lifted my hair up and kissed the nape of my neck. I liked that well enough, though it tickled. Then I felt him raise up once more, and I worried that he would want to leave. Then I worried that he wouldn't. Again I thought, *I ought to get away now.*

But no; he only took hold of my hips, then he raised them a little. It seemed to me an awfully awkward, embarrassing position; I wondered what strange new thing he had in mind. I glanced back over my shoulder and saw he'd unfastened his own trousers, too. He was kneeling above me, naked as the man from my daydream, the same tan skin and dark hair. Except, I reminded myself, all this was real.

Then he lay on top of me again. And he pushed himself into me, hard.

The pain wasn't as bad as when I'd cut my forehead on the tiller a few weeks earlier. It wasn't nearly as bad as my aching muscles after a long day lifting pots or tonging down in a deep bed. But it was *where* it hurt, that first awful tearing feel inside, and my silly, helpless position that made me cry out. When I did, though, he didn't stop but only shoved my head down and whispered a long string of shocking words into my ear. Some were love words, I think, and some so filthy I couldn't understand at first what he meant and wouldn't repeat them even now. But after a moment, my body seemed to know, somehow, exactly what the words were and what he wanted of me.

Once or twice I had seen a few farm animals having to do with each other. Mostly our hogs and Dad's dogs. I had heard the cats moaning and squalling in the middle of the night. And years earlier, on a shopping trip to the shore, we passed a field and I glimpsed a horse astride a mare, gripping her shoulders with his forelegs as he pounded away at her. My parents had looked away so fast, had gone suddenly so tight-lipped I'd known better than to ask. But as a child it had been hard to relate such doings to people, even after Tommy Kellum had gathered a few of us on the playground at school one afternoon and whispered his notions about the strange games our parents got up to at night while we slept.

"You're a liar, Tommy Kellum," I had said, though I was worried he might be right. It would explain certain parts of a great puzzle. But I couldn't willingly believe Mam and Dad could ever do such things to each other.

"Well, how do you think you got here, then?" he'd asked triumphantly. And of course I couldn't answer that.

So part of me said no to all this and meant to get up and run, or at least squirm away from the hurt. But Nathan stroked my back and between my legs, and instead of escaping, I was pulling at my shirt, tugging it up as he whispered encouragement. His hands slid up to grip my breasts and rub and pinch my nipples, and all the while he kept pushing in and out of me.

So finally I knew how it all felt. But I still didn't know how to take in the idea that this thing was happening to me, Annie Revels, on the beach in broad daylight.

Had I done something I shouldn't have, or said something, been misunderstood? Somehow I must have agreed to all this strange business. It was what the pigs did; the rooster in the yard mounted the hens this way. But they were animals, and this was the nameless sin I had heard the minister warn of, and those Sundays there was always more squirming and throat clearing in the pews. I finally had to admit in my heart and to the ghost of poor, dead Tommy Kellum that my parents must have done the same to make me and Rebecca and the dead brother who lay under the beach grass. Yet I still could not picture them sweating and grunting and moaning, my weathered and gray-headed parents; jamming parts of their bodies into each other, as hard and frantic as we were then, with no notion of shame or of stopping, even for a moment. No, this had to be different, somehow. Surely it was unnatural.

So I pushed my face into the checkered picnic cloth in shame. I bit down on the thick oilcloth and buried my face in its rubbery dryness as Nathan slammed into me, breathing harder. Until for a moment he paused, and I heard him shout out something. Then he collapsed onto my back again, his sweating chest glued to my bare skin.

The world seemed very quiet after that. I wondered if he'd fainted, or gone to sleep, or even died somehow. I worried that, judging from the throbbing hurt between my legs, we might be stuck together there.

But then, with one last shudder and gasp, he rolled off and away from me.

Surely that was my best chance to get up and run, as he lay with his eyes closed, panting. But I didn't. By then I couldn't believe my knees would still bend, that my legs would rise up and carry me. So I lay quiet, face hidden in the cloth. Waiting for the next surprising thing.

After a moment, I heard him sigh, and felt his hands on me. Then I was afraid it might be starting up all over again, but he only turned me over to face him and gently pulled all my clothing back into place. He tied the belt on my father's old trousers and buttoned my work shirt up to my neck, apologizing when one button popped off and disappeared in the sand. He wiped the sweat from my face with a finger and kissed my nose again quickly. Then, more slowly, my mouth.

The most surprising thing to me was that after Nathan Combs stood and tucked in his shirt and ran his fingers through his thick black hair, he looked exactly the same as he had back in the boat, before we set foot on Steamer Island. And he acted as if nothing had changed or was different between us. He leaned down and combed the hair back from my face with his fingers. Then he patted my shoulder and held out a hand. The expression on his face was so confident, so reasonable, that I took hold and let him pull me to my feet. He actually whistled as we walked back out to the beached boat, me stumbling alongside, him swinging the empty picnic hamper.

I felt numb, or as if I had suddenly gone stark raving crazy.

And yet, hadn't I wanted it to happen? I'm sure I must have, though I hadn't guessed how truly strange, how awkward, and how complicated it would all be.

Just before we reached his launch, I stumbled into a sand hollow full of broken eggshells, an abandoned skimmer nest. He dropped the basket and caught me up as tenderly as a father would a toddling baby. I think I flinched then at his touch, but he didn't seem to notice. He kissed the top of my head and lifted me over the gunwale into the boat. I sat on the thwart, staring at him dumbly.

What can I say now? I wondered.

But he only smiled, gave me the pleased look of a whisker-licking cat, and shoved the skiff in one smooth motion out into the water.

We motored back to my boat, where the empty crab pots still sat jumbled like a child's toy blocks in the bow. Where he handed me in and bid me good-bye. Where I, too, sat for a long time after he left, before I could gather my wits enough to recall I needed to hoist the canvas again and set sail for home, wondering all the while if I'd lost my mind. Only sure that such things had really happened to me because of the ache between my thighs and the stinging scrape where his beard had sanded the skin between my shoulders.

A bit later came one last unarguable proof; a warm trickle between my legs I felt and wondered at, since my time of the month was yet far off. I slid a hand into my trousers, and when I looked at my fingers I saw on them some white, pearly stuff sparkling in the afternoon sun, sticky as cane syrup. So then I knew that warm, slow seeping down my thighs was also a part of it, the last of Nathan's strange gift. I sniffed my fingertips and wrinkled my nose a bit at the mixed salt-and-bleach scent. Then I took hold of the tiller again and guided the trawler back up the channel and through the marshes to Yaupon Island.

*   *   *

I thought these several new things over all that night and the next day. If I forgot for a few moments, I had only to press my legs together for the soreness to remind me of my boldness and my folly. This was exactly the sort of wickedness hinted at in clusters of whispering women and warned against in sermons, though the nature of the sin never seemed to really be described in any detail. I knew it was wrong, for who could I ever tell? A good girl, a decent one who attended to churchgoing, the Bible, and her parents' teachings at home, would never have been out on that island alone and naked one time, much less again, with a man.

Yet I couldn't make myself feel sorry. I was near twenty and not at all pretty. As far as I knew, no one had ever desired me before. But now I had Nathan Combs to think of nights when I rolled over under the covers, instead of just my own clever fingers. Yes, I would soon be twenty and no doubt an old maid. But at least I knew what it was like now to share my body, if not my bed, with a man.

True, I hadn't enjoyed all the sweaty frantic thrusting nearly as much as he had seemed to. But I couldn't deny that thinking of Nathan and the things he had done made me grope at myself more often now in the dark, and it was harder to muffle my sudden cries of pleasure in the pillow. Sometimes I would gasp or moan, and through a mist of sweat see my sister turn and frown in her sleep. In her narrow bed she mumbled fretful words I couldn't make out. I would hold still then, hold my breath until she sighed herself back to sleep.

I began to carry enough food for two with me each morning when I left. Oh, it was silly, but sometimes I pretended I was married to Nathan and coming out to bring him lunch the way a wife would. I worried we'd meet again, then worried myself nearly sick that we wouldn't. One morning a week later, we did, and at this second meeting, I wasn't surprised or hurt when, after a few kisses and caresses, he laid me down right there in the big motor launch. That time, as he unfastened my trousers, escape was the last thing on my mind.

We met several times a week, sometimes by plan, sometimes not. If I encountered him on the water and he was alone, we usually went back to Steamer Island. He seemed to like it there, though with all the sand and mosquitos, I couldn't see why. Or sometimes we visited a big old dilapidated duck blind, a stilted wooden hut large enough for us to stretch out in on a blanket. Once, a boatload of tourists came by, and once, a cargo of schoolchildren on a nature trip. We held still, our hands sealing each other's mouths, trying not to laugh aloud as their teacher commented in city accents on the possible uses of the ramshackle wooden structure we hid in.

When we were exhausted and had time to talk, we mostly spoke of things other than ourselves. We talked

about fishing, about the increase in tourists and the de-
crease in black ducks. He said he wanted to build a house
someday on one of these islands. That if he hadn't gone off
to the war, he'd have done it by now.

So he had been, like Tommy. But he had come back.
"Where all did you go, over there?" I asked. "What did you
do?" I wondered if he had ever killed anyone but couldn't
think how to ask a person a thing such as that.

His jaw tightened up, and I thought for a moment he
wouldn't answer me at all. He looked angry, and I thought
he was mad at me for asking. But then he only shrugged
and rubbed the skin on my bare arm. "Well, France. Laid
in a lot of muddy ditches while the Huns shot at us. Spent
some time in Italy, too." I waited, but that was all he would
say about it, that time.

I told him I had a family, though I didn't mention that
my sister at home was younger, and beautiful. Later at
night I always thought of a million questions I had really
wanted to ask: Where had he been born? Who were his
folks? Did he have any kin hereabouts? But somehow, during the short time we had together, all I could think of was
quickly shedding my clothes, and his, too.

He wore no ring, and I refused to think about the possibility of a wife. Most of Cobb's guides were young men,
though Dad had mentioned a few had families who lived
in cottages on the island. Because Nathan wore no band,
nor did he carry the telltale mark of one on his finger, I
decided he was unmarried. I feared to ask outright, though.

I couldn't stand to imagine otherwise. Sometimes at night, yawning and finally tired of touching myself, I'd say a shameful prayer to ensure that he was one of the single men there at Cobb's.

After two months or so, I started to plot ways to bring Nathan home with me. He hadn't mentioned any desire to come, but he hadn't said anything against it, either. I sometimes pictured him at the kitchen table, eating a good dinner I had cooked myself. Mam and Rebecca on one side of the table, Nathan and I across from them, holding hands, our thighs pressed secretly together, our legs entangled under the table. My bare foot, catlike, rubbing his ankle.

One day, he brought me back with him to Cobb's Island, though we didn't get out of the boat. We sat in it not far from the shucking house. Screaming gulls wheeled in midair, fighting and cussing each other over the guts and head of a drumfish catch.

I decided at last to ask.

"I wondered—I mean, I thought you might like to have some dinner with us one night," I said, keeping my voice low, careful to sound unconcerned. I wiped sweating hands on my pants when I saw he'd glanced away. "You know. With my family."

He looked back at me, neither smiling nor frowning, and my stomach churned. "You don't have to come," I said quickly.

"What are they like?" he asked. "Your family."

"It'll be just my mother and sister," I said quickly. "I told you that. My father died last year."

Suddenly, I feared the whole idea was a mistake. What would happen when he met dotty old Mam? When he got a look at my much prettier little sister?

"Anyway, they're very shy," I said. "Mam is old. Rebecca is . . ."

I paused, thinking, *Leave it go. Don't say another word.*

But of course my mouth worked on, oblivious to any warning by good sense. A lie seemed a small price to keep what I had already begun to think of as mine. "My sister's a little . . . well, not right in the head."

Now, it was true Rebecca acted a bit strange at times, even I could see that. We'd been raised without having much to do with other folks; we'd developed our own ways and notions. But she wasn't loony; that was a terrible, bald lie. All I know is at that moment I needed to make myself into something better, to be sure I could keep Nathan all to myself. I felt ashamed, too. For Granny Jester had predicted this. Mam's sharp words and hard looks had told me all along that I would grow up to do bad things.

Yet in the end, I found I still didn't care. This was not like being Tommy Kellum's girl; it wasn't pretend, it was real. Nathan had chosen me for me, not as a way to get to my sister. He seemed to like my looks just fine. So I didn't give a damn if he thought my sister was a two-headed freak, as long as I could keep seeing him. I would not share him. I just would not.

It would have been safer, I realized then, to simply not bring him home. Yet I wanted that, too. I wanted it all.

So I waited for Nathan's answer. He frowned a little but then only said, "I guess, sure." Then, smiling a bit, "Well, why not? It might be nice."

So I took a bold step even farther away from God's truth.

"My mother, she and my sister, I mean. They don't go out, don't see folks much. So I thought—seeing the way they are—maybe it'd be best to tell them you're a friend of Dad's. That you've been away and met me out here and just found out he's passed away."

He frowned again, as if considering this new complication that was part of me. Then he squeezed my hand. "All right, if that's what you want."

I was surprised he agreed so readily to deceit. But I was relieved when he nodded, as if we both had decided it was all fine. That telling lies was the normal way to introduce folks you invited to dinner.

Seven

To make dinner for Nathan I sacrificed a bushel of very fine Jimmy crabs that should have gone to the buy boats and made us money for over the winter. I decided I would also feed him fresh August runner beans, and make biscuits along with whipped sweet potatoes drizzled with molasses. I'd already considered and rejected fried chicken. For several days I'd debated salt ham or fresh pork. I had eyed the lean flanks of our rangy old hogs so often they began to roll their eyes and scramble away, as if they saw the ghost of a butchering knife in my hand.

So I'd finally decided on crab cakes made from the choicest bits of backfin meat and fried in butter. I'd bathe myself and dress after getting everything ready to cook. One jar of preserves from the winter last still sat on the pantry shelf, so we could have persimmon cake for dessert.

What seemed strange was that for the first time I would wear a dress in front of Nathan. I wanted him to see me differently, at least this once. Maybe as another person, not just the disheveled, hard-handed woman who worked and sweated out on the water—though he seemed to like that woman well enough. But I wondered what might happen if I appeared more a lady for a change, than one of the men who worked out on the boats.

I wondered, and I worried over everything for days.

The morning of the dinner, as we sat in the kitchen eating breakfast, my sister stared at me across the table.

"My, Annie. You look mighty pale," she said. "You feeling sickly today?"

I looked at my eggs and avoided her gaze. "I'm fine. Only tired, maybe."

I wished I could blot out the sight of her smooth skin and perfect face just for one day. My nose was peeling, my summer freckles so thick they nearly connected on my face by then. And a new pip-ginny, red and sore, had come up by the corner of my mouth.

She came on me later that afternoon as I looked in the hall mirror at that damned red bump decorating my chin, at the dry, frizzled ends of my hair. Staring at myself as if taking inventory of a stranger. It gave me a start when the delicate oval of her face floated into view, ghostlike, beside my own plain, square-jawed one. I looked dark as an Indian next to Rebecca, and that, rather than startlement, had more to do with me snapping at her.

"Don't ever dare sneak up on me that way."

"Sorry," she said, looking at me with a little smile. "I thought you seen me come up behind you."

"Well, I didn't."

"You know, Annie," she said, still gazing at me thoughtfully. "It wouldn't exactly disfurnish you to buy a few nice pins, or some tortoise combs for your hair."

I rolled my eyes at that. A lot of good such things would do me out on the water, in the sun and wind and rain.

But still she stood there, not moving. I wondered if perhaps she enjoyed making me feel ugly. But then she reached up and smoothed my hair back the way Mam used to do when I was little. Then she gathered it all behind my ears and swept it above my collar in a sort of twist.

"You know," she said again, "if you would go by me, I could show you how to guss this old mane up. It's nice and thick. You'd look pretty, Annie, and stylish, too, with it all piled on top of your head."

I held in a shiver. Her hands felt nice stroking on my hair; I could almost have sunk down and curled up on the rug, purring like the old cat. I leaned back against her a bit, the comfortable way we'd stood sometimes as kids, and our gazes met in the mirror. She made a silly face and we both laughed. But then I recalled why my hair mattered at all and straightened up, worried. Could she know, somehow, about Nathan?

"It's all the go these days, truly," she wheedled, turning my head this way and that.

Finally I snorted and pulled away. "Aye, I'd look a fool," I said. But then I wondered. "No, more like it'd only show off the huck on the back of my neck."

"Oh, Annie. Your neck is all clean," she protested, not seeing I was joking.

In any case, once she got hold of an idea, my sister was a true hardhead. So at last I let her fuss with my hair, for the first time, thinking it might not hurt. That I might look prettier to Nathan. I'd at least look different.

Maybe I didn't know much about fashion, but I had known for ages how to make good crab cakes, for we ate the catch of the day as often as not at home. Still, after Rebecca was done fussing with water and combs and had put so many pins in my head it felt like a sewing cushion, I hunted through bins and boxes for Mam's old cookbook. I finally found *The Methodical Cook* on the bookshelf, a slim, faded book with missing and dog-eared pages, the cover splotched with stains and drippings. I read her favorite recipe over carefully, slowly, as if it were printed in French and I had to translate all by myself.

I read it in a whisper. "One pound of cooked backfin. A half cup of crumbs. Two eggs. A large pinch of salt and a small one of pepper. A dash of cayenne."

I repeated it in my head a third time like a singsongy witch's spell. Just before dinnertime I would form soft balls of the crabmeat mixture in my hands, then flatten and fry

them gently, until they turned a perfect golden brown outside and were hot all the way through.

I put the ingredients aside and sat at the table, thinking.
I had already told Rebecca I'd run into an old friend of
Dad's the day before, on a trip to the docks to sell crabs to
the buy boats. I didn't tell her he was young and handsome.
So, like as not, she was expecting some musty, crusty
codger we'd have to shout at so he could hear us. She'd
already suggested we'd better leave an empty coffee can
close by so he could spit his wad of chew into it before
grace.

Lord knows we'd had to do that very thing the few times
Dad had invited any waterman he knew into the house for
a hot meal. Our father had liked a dab of Red Man himself,
when he felt he could afford it. Mam had at least trained
him to rid himself of the stuff before meals. Though Nathan would smoke once in a while, he had never smelled
of old plug or stale, cheap tobacco. No dried brown patches
of juicy spit marred his clothes. There was nothing of the
codger about him. But I kept quiet and silently handed her
an empty Maxwell House can.

I didn't tell Mam anything at all. I figured there was no
point to it.

An hour before Nathan was due, I turned away from the stove
and suddenly saw, as if for the first time, the place where
we lived.

The house was not large, only a timbered cottage Dad had built for Mam just before they married. His older brothers had been living then, and they'd helped carpenter it, because the groom's kin always builds the house and furniture in these parts. All oystermen, like their fathers before them, they'd worked for days on end axing lumber for the shell of the house. The framework was thick pine timbers and had withstood thirty-five years of flood tides, hurricanes, and northeasters. The inside they'd paneled in light pine planks, but years of cooking grease and the smoke from Dad's pipe had darkened it to a gloomy brown. The tops and corner of the rough-hewn tables were smooth now from decades of use, and the huge four-poster made of the same framing poles would have slept an elephant safely. But it all must still look cheap and rustic and crude if a body was used to store-bought stuff.

Mam's family, the Jesters, contributed household goods, the women sewing and crocheting for weeks before the ceremony. Mam had had some nice things, pieced quilts and lace crocheted curtains and tablecloths. But she had long ago stopped caring for them, and now I saw all the old patches and the newer unpatched holes. The veils of cobweb in the corners, the yellowed cotton lace, the grimy edges of the curtains that drooped at our windows. My days held barely enough time to pull pots and check lines, maintain the boat, and grow a few vegetables out back. When could I ever have a moment to sit and crochet and mend and sew? Besides, I had hated doing any of those things the few times I'd tried. To sit still and finger a tiny needle in and out of a slippery piece of cloth made me feel cross-eyed and screamy.

But working for the Cobbs, Nathan would be used to being among fine things. True, he'd taken me as I was, dirty, ragged, wearing men's pants, and shamefully often no drawers, and never complained. Yet now I wanted things different. Wanted him to be impressed with my womanly skills, my still-slender young shape in Mam's good blue-patterned silk dress. I'd pulled it from the closet and shaken the wrinkles out, hoping in the evening light he wouldn't notice a moth hole or two.

The Cobbs of Cobb's Island had started out as fishermen, rougher than my family had ever been, according to Granny Jester and Mam. Granny even claimed that they'd lived in tents and driftwood sheds at first, and cooked over bonfires on the beach, and sometimes scavenged like wreckers. Though when she'd said so, Dad had rolled his eyes and said, "Now, Mother Jester."

But Nathan worked for them now, and these were their prosperous days. How poor and dark and musty this place would seem to him! As I paced the house, not sure where to start or what to do, I thought I could even smell a dank whiff of stale piss coming from Mam's room. She once in a while wet the bed now, because she didn't wake up in time for us to get her to the privy.

I collapsed on Dad's old hassock, ready to bawl, and its rusty springs squealed at me like a wounded rabbit.

Just then Rebecca came down the hall and walked past, wearing an old flowered wrapper of Mam's.

"Are you insane," I cried, balling my hands into fists because for a moment I almost wanted to hit her. "It's suppertime, and you look like you just dragged out of the bed."

She stared at me as if she knew well enough who was crazy and who wasn't. "I was on my way from the privy, going to right now change," she mumbled and hurried off.

I called after her, "And make sure Mam wears something decent to the table."

Nathan arrived just as it was getting dark out.

I'd set the persimmon cake on the windowsill to cool and had just started heating the skillet for the crab cakes on the old cast-iron stove. When I heard his knock, I wiped my hands quickly on my apron, then sniffed my fingers and realized that, as usual, I would smell of seafood when we met.

I opened the door slowly, not wanting him to know how I'd rushed across the room to get there.

"Come in," I said, but instead he grabbed my arm and drew me out onto the stoop. He wrapped his arms around me tight and kissed my mouth hard. Then backed away a step, and turned his palms up, empty. "That's all I brought," he said, grinning. "A mighty poor excuse for a guest."

As if that mattered. I laughed and took his hand, pulling him inside.

Rebecca came into the living room. Just as I was about

to introduce them, she gasped, "Lord-a-mercy, Annie, what's that smell?"

I had forgotten the cast-iron pan on the stove. I'd left it there to heat with nothing in it but a little grease. The smoke was bad when I ran into the kitchen, and it took me a while to wipe the blackened iron clean and set things to rights again. At least I hadn't burned the dinner.

When I came back into the living room, Rebecca and Nathan were on the sofa, at opposite ends. Her face was flushed, and though he was only looking polite and nodding, I didn't like the way she was talking thirty to the dozen, waving her hands around. I'd never seen her act so lively, or her color so high and pretty. Was he hanging on her words because I'd told him she was slow, not right in the head, and he wanted to be sure he understood? Oh, why, why had I told him that? Or did he already think, secretly, that she was the Sermon on the Mount and the Gettysburg Address all rolled into one neat package?

Just before he looked up and saw me, he reached over, and for one heart-stalling second, I thought he would stroke her fine black hair, long and shiny and glowing in the light of the oil lamps. But he only smacked a mosquito buzzing on the wall above her head.

Then he saw I'd come back and got up slowly. He didn't look as if he'd done anything wrong; he seemed right glad to see me.

But still I wondered.

"Annie," he said, grinning again. "I mean, Miss Revels."

"Mr. Combs," I said back, a bit sharp, then smiled to show I was joking. I told Rebecca to get Mam set up at her place while I finished up and got things on the table. She made a face but got up anyway. I wanted Nathan to notice how smooth I handled everything at home. That I wasn't really just that big rangy girl with rough-calloused hands and a sun-baked face and arm muscles like any waterman's. I could do wifely things, too. Could even look like a woman a man might want to marry.

But when I glanced his way again, I wondered if he was noticing Rebecca's backside, the snaky sway of her hips as she left the room. I went back to the kitchen and slid the crab cakes careful out of the pan. I dumped the sweet potato biscuits hastily on a plate, not noticing until after I'd done it that the china was chipped and stained, so I had to go and get another. By then I felt altogether frantic. I didn't want to leave them out there with just dotty old Mam for a chaperon.

I burnt my finger on the pot lid when I lifted it to check the runner beans. My face was beaded with sweat, my armpits soaked, too. I rushed to the table and piled things blindly onto the cloth.

"Can't I lend a hand?" asked Nathan, rising halfway from his chair.

"No," I snapped again. Then, when I saw his bewildered expression, I made myself say more softly, "Well, yes. Please. Can you carry the platter out?"

So, after that, I kept him in the kitchen with me, even

though I felt it was not in the truest sense a man's place. Though this made little sense when I thought about it. I hadn't minded when Dad had cooked, and he'd seemed to enjoy it, too. But perhaps he had only been trying not to seem bitter about Mam's infirmity. With her sick, he'd had to do for us in the kitchen, until I'd taken over. Unlike Mam, I didn't need the help. But at least I could keep an eye on Nathan. Whether he needed watching or not was beside the point to my shaking hands and anxious, circular thoughts.

But why did I need to bird-dog him? I wondered. He paid me attention all the time when we were out on the water or on the island, or hid away in a duck blind or a fishing shack. When we were alone together. So what if he did act nice to my family, or even compliment my baby sister? After all, he had his part to act out in our little charade. I had seen to that.

At dinner he was charming to everyone. Even Mam perked up and seemed to take in what he said to her. The words were what I'd schooled him to say, since he never really knew my father.

"Now, when you come over," I'd told him, "be sure to comment on the kitchen chairs. Dad made them special for Mam, and she was always right proud of his carpenter skills."

"I won't forget," he'd said, his voice muffled as he nuzzled my neck and stroked my naked back. He'd made me smile then, rehearsing his lines between kisses.

And when he repeated those things to Mam, she smiled, too. Her cheeks pinked. She watched his mouth as he talked, his fine-carved lips, and her face glowed nearly as bright as Rebecca's. I relaxed a bit then. Plainly Nathan had an effect on all women. Some men just did. He couldn't help what he'd been born with, like blue eyes or a dimple.

That was why I loved him. For the way he was.

I paused with a fork full of crab cake halfway to my mouth. I loved Nathan; could that be right?

As I sat and ate my own good food, I turned that notion over and over in my head like a curious-shaped bit of sea glass. Wasn't sure I liked it, exactly, or that it was pretty to look at. The notion that I loved him for the way he made me *feel*. It sounded trivial, selfish somehow. I never heeded Granny Jester's old warning or Mam's scolding judgments when I was with him. I only thought of myself, of the pleasure I could have with his body and with mine.

So yes, I did love him for the way it made me feel. I had to wonder then if I would want him so much if he had never yet touched me. Or if we couldn't meet anymore out on the water, what would happen then?

The food had turned out right nicely, I could see he was enjoying it. And it felt good, somehow, not at all awkward, to wear my mother's old best dress and have my hair all pinned up. For hours that night, I was sure I wasn't ugly. My rough, sunburned hands even looked smaller, finer, more skilled and capable. I thought in those moments I could come to terms with all the worries and trials of life if I could just keep Nathan Combs with me for the rest of my days.

After we finished our cake, he pushed back from the table. "Never had a finer meal, Miss Revels. Not even at Cobb's Island Hotel."

"You can't eat another slice of Annie's good persimmon cake?" asked Rebecca, tilting her head the same birdlike way Mam often did. "You can't go away saying, 'Those Revels women are chinchy,' if I offer, anyhow."

"No thank you, Miss Revels. I've run ashore," said Nathan. But he was smiling at me, not her.

I started picking up plates, looking down at the table to hide my own growing smile. "You are surely a smooth talker, Mr. Combs."

He insisted he'd do dishes with my sister and give me a well-earned rest.

"Why, thanks. But I don't need help." He would see now, I could do it all. The evening was going so well, I suddenly felt generous. I would leave them in the parlor while I cleaned up. I didn't need to keep tabs on them. "And Becca needs to sit with Mam. Our mother gets nervous when she's left alone too long. Isn't that so, Rebecca?"

It was true enough. Mam might not have a bad migraine for months; her leg might not trouble her for weeks, if the weather was dry. It was her mind that we could rarely rely on. She'd seem sharp as a scaling knife one day, then next thing you knew, she'd be in some past world, with folks no one else could see anymore but her.

One foggy night she'd gone right out the door looking for Dad, even though we reminded her almost every day he'd been dead and gone for a year. Even though earlier that same day we'd walked her over to his grave, as we did once a week at least. To put a Mason jar of flowers on it, and straighten the cross. When she'd slipped out later, it was raining, no moon, and we'd had the very devil of a time to find her and bring her back, shivering with damp, muddled in her mind, but safe at least.

"Well then," said my sister. "Why don't you take a rest, Annie, and sit with her? I think you worked so hard on that good dinner, we ought to clean up. Don't you agree, Mr. Combs?"

I had a prick of foreboding then. I frowned at Rebecca, but she wasn't looking at me. I tried to catch Nathan's eye, to shake my head, but he nodded slowly and seriously at Rebecca, as if it was natural she decide this. So there was nothing else I could say without looking the fool.

Nathan helped Mam up, took her arm real gentlemanly, and led her to the sofa. Rebecca disappeared into the kitchen. And a dark thought came into my head like a song and stuck there.

You bitch. You little bitch.

Angry or not, I had never thought such words about my sister before. I felt my face heating with shame; I felt my good dinner turning over in my stomach. My own sister. But still I repeated them over and over in my mind to block out the sea chanty Mam was singing, one she always liked

to hum or sing a verse of over and over till it made a body
want to scream or stuff her poor old mouth with rags.

> *O I thought I heard the old man say*
> *Leave her, Johnny, leave her*
> *For you know you're bound to leave her.*

Tonight the lyrics, especially, played on my last nerve.
But I sat, tired of her quavery soprano and trying not to
hate her. Trying without getting up from the sofa to every
once in a while peer around the corner into the kitchen. I
smelled the clean scent of soap. Heard the clank of the
hand pump, the splash of water into the deep sink, the
clink of glass on china, the low murmur of voices. But I
was too proud to get up, and of course no one can see
around a corner. Though now and then, I heard them
laughing.

I should have told her, I thought. Just told her flat out
before he came that Nathan was mine. She is my sister,
after all, and we're grown now. She can't expect to just
have him, like a doll or a storybook. My own fault, my
punishment for telling lies about my family.

I suppose I still might have gotten up, gone in there for
a moment. Or even glanced in from the doorway; Mam
didn't need me right at her side like a sheepdog. But I
couldn't. Or rather, I resolved that I wouldn't.

Later, when Mam was nodding off on the sofa, I called
Rebecca from the kitchen to put her to bed. I took the

dishcloth from Nathan silently and started drying the last plate. But he pulled cloth and plate from me and set them on the counter. I opened my mouth to object; we weren't finished yet. But he laid one blunt finger against my lips. I had to smile at the familiar feel of his skin against my mouth.

"What's out there?" He pointed out the kitchen window, where the moonlight shone on the shed out back.

"Only some old tools and the wringer washer."

"Oh. And what's in here?" The door he meant led to the storage place. Granny Jester's old bedroom.

"Nothing much," I said. "Well, odds and ends. Pantry things. Old chairs. Boxes. Nothing you want to see in there."

"No?"

He took hold of my wrist and laid his other hand on the knob. That door had always been sticky, the wood warped and swelled with humidity. But that night it worked for him just as smooth as glass; I would have sworn for a moment that it opened of its own accord.

He leaned to look inside.

I hung back. "There's no light."

He tugged at my arm. "There's a moon. We don't need one."

I hesitated. Hadn't stepped inside there too often lately, except in broad daylight, I'd sometimes dash in and grab a jar of preserves, or a spare blanket, or an old crate. To me, on hot, damp days, it still smelled of sickness, of my granny's sad craziness. I didn't much care to go now, and so I balked.

But Nathan turned and scooped me up like a child. Carried me in and shut the door firmly behind us.

It wasn't as dark as all that. By the bright moonlit square of window, the dusty room looked silvery and drowned, as if we were swimming under gray water speckled with floating spawn. I smelled mold and old rotting cloth and something oversweet and sticky, like old apples. I smelled Nathan close by me, clean sweat and sugary tobacco and lemon soap from the dishes.

He set me down and unbuttoned the front of my dress. Gently circled my throat with his hands, stroked it with his thumbs, then moved slowly down over my collarbone, my breasts, and my stomach. I was amazed again at the smoothness of his palms—at least compared to mine, so horn-rough and cracked, the nails busted and torn. The dusty air of the room was so cool, and his mouth so hot on my skin, it kept me shivering.

He lifted his head, looked around. Then hooked his boot around the leg of a broken-spindled chair and dragged it over.

"Wait," I said. "What if . . ."

He sat on the chair and set me astride his lap, facing him. Fumbled with buttons and zippers and the elastic of my last pair of good drawers. With his warm lips on my cold face, his tongue filling my mouth, I couldn't speak. Didn't want to, either.

Once, over his shoulder, I thought I saw a pale shape floating, and I held my breath, wondering if it could be a ghost; Granny, or even Tommy Kellum, come to see how shamelessly wicked a person I truly was. Or worse, a living white face pressed to the window glass. But Nathan gripped my thighs and lifted me a little, then set me back down again, slowly, slowly, and after that I didn't care if Rebecca or Mam or Tommy or my dead Granny herself was watching and judging us.

It had hurt the first time Nathan had laid me down beneath him, there on the island. Of course, I hadn't quite known what all would happen, either. Afterwards, I always knew very well what to expect, and looked forward to it. I liked his nearness, his hands on me, the heat of his skin under mine, and the way he kissed my face after. But I could tell it wasn't the same for me as for him; he seemed to get lost in what we were doing. As if he couldn't stop, even if he wanted to.

This time was different. As he held my waist and I moved in his lap, my cold shiver warmed, and a strange shudder slowly took my body. Gradual at first, yet finally so strong it wouldn't let me even take a deep breath until I grabbed hold of his shoulders and drove him deeper into me. I ground my hips so hard the worn glue joints of that old chair groaned and creaked like a little boat in a black squall. And this time, I could press my face into Nathan's warm, live shoulder, instead of a pillow, to muffle my cries.

*   *   *

We'd only come out of the pantry and been in the kitchen a minute or so when Rebecca came in, too. She looked pale and upset and seemed out of breath.

"What's wrong?" I asked.

She wouldn't look straight at me. "Oh . . . Mam was a handful tonight. You see," she said, turning to Nathan, "her mind's sort of catabiased. She can't help it, poor old thing."

I glanced at him and saw he looked a little startled. I noticed, too, that his top shirt button was still undone.

I willed my sister to excuse herself and run off to bed, but she kept on.

"Really, can you believe it, Mr. Combs? Mam kept wanting me to come out and get you. 'It's so late,' she kept saying. 'Tell your father to come to bed and get some rest.' She pestered me no end. Isn't that funny? I swear she thinks you're *Dad*." I heard a strange quaver in her voice at the end. She didn't really sound all that amused.

Nathan shrugged and laughed politely, looking a bit lost at the direction of the conversation. "Well," he said finally, "at least I know one lady in the house looks kindly on me."

I led him to the front door, the inside of my thighs sticky, legs still trembling. I felt I could barely move that short distance across the floor.

"Good night, Mr. Combs," called Rebecca from behind us, her voice too loud.

Nathan held my hand at the door before he turned away.

Only later, waiting for my sister to come back from her turn at the privy, did I notice the taste of bitter copper in my mouth. In Granny's old room, I'd chewed the inside of my lip bloody, trying to keep quiet.

All that fall, Nathan came to dinner every week or so. When he left, it felt all wrong. While he was with us, I had to shove my hands in my pockets to keep from touching him, to bite down on the side of my cheek to remember not to kiss him right at the table. I wanted so bad to keep him there. I dreamed once or twice we'd married, and even began to think of that possibility during the day. He never brought it up, though. I wondered why but never asked, maybe for fear I wouldn't like the answer. Besides, that would mean keeping him near Rebecca, too. Yet how could I move away to Cobb's Island or anywhere else? She and Mam would starve or worse.

So I decided it was best that way. We still met out on the water, though he was busier now with fall and duck-hunting season. I'd see him at a distance sometimes, ferrying boatloads of hunters. Some of them looked experienced, some held their double-barrels awkwardly as furled umbrellas as they bobbed in the autumn chop.

There were never enough duck blinds this time of year, so the guides towed out more of the heavy wooden sink-boxes and anchored them at various spots around the marshes. Sometimes Nathan would bring a few sportsmen out to one, then run them back to Cobb's Island and pick me up after. We'd lie in the same box where a few hours earlier tourists had crouched, waiting to kill something on the wing.

We were nearly caught one afternoon by old Cobb himself, who sailed past in a beat-up catboat. When I noticed him just a few yards off, I was sure he'd seen us.

Nathan said not to worry. "The old man's deaf, and pretty near blind."

"Then how's he get about on the water?" I demanded.

"By smell," he said, as he dragged me down again.

Eight

One night in early December I put dinner on the table, but my
mother and sister didn't come. I looked and called and finally found Mam in her room, alone. I found her slippers
under the bed and put them on her cold bare feet, then
brought her out to the usual place. My sister still didn't
appear.

"Where's Rebecca?" I asked, after I'd pushed Mam's
chair up close.

She didn't answer, only patted her napkin and picked up
her fork. So I called down the hall again and then outside,
though it was so chilly I couldn't believe Becca would just
go out for a walk. Her shawl was on the hook by the door,
anyhow. I went back to the table and sat down across from
Mam. I noticed she had set down the fork and held her
tatting bobbin in her hands. Though she couldn't make lace

anymore, she liked to hold it, especially when she was up-set.

"Mam, haven't you seen Rebecca?"

She shook her head again. "Something wrong with that girl."

"Oh, so you just now noticed," I joked. "And here I al-ways thought she was born that way."

Mam glanced at me sideways. Her eyes looked bright, clearer than usual. "Won't last a good high water," she said.

"What won't, Mam?" I started slicing the bread. But then the front door banged open, and Rebecca dragged in, shivering, no jacket or sweater or shawl.

"Come now, maid, are you crazy?" I said. "It's cold enough to make your blood hum out there."

She didn't answer, just slumped into her chair at the table without a word and stared down at her plate.

I helped Mam scoot up closer so she wouldn't spill things.

"Ah, livers," she said in a delighted voice. Though Mam seemed not too sharp on most things by then, she still liked her food well enough.

I served Rebecca, too, and sat down again, across from her, but she didn't look up.

"Something wrong?" I asked.

No answer. So I looked around to see if anyone else wanted to say grace, then murmured, "Bless this food to the use of our bodies for your greater glory and in your name. Amen."

I picked up my knife and fork, cut a steaming chicken liver in half, and heard a retching sound. I laid the knife aside and looked up at my sister, gagging over her plate. "Mercy, Becca. You're having a bad go. Got the flu?"

"No." She shoved her chair back from the table, away from the hot pile of grayish livers lumped on her plate.

"Poor sis," I said, chewing slowly. I felt sorry for her, almost motherly, she looked so ill. "Want some calamus tea? Why don't you lie down, and I'll—"

"I don't want to lie down," she snapped. She got up but then just stood beside her chair, not moving.

"What in heaven's name is wrong with you?" I asked. I took another bite and chewed it slowly, watching her.

"It's good," said Mam, nodding and smacking her lips.

"Now don't smack, honey," I said, wiping her chin like a child's. "Use your napkin." I glanced up at my sister again. "I mean it. What is it that's got into you, Rebecca?"

She stared at me as if I had sprouted fins or a tail. Then gradually her face took on a different look. Her eyes got narrow, and she had a funny kind of knowing smile that barely stretched her mouth. All too crafty for my little sister Rebecca.

"Oh," she said. "I thought for a minute you knew."

"Knew what?" I sighed, tired of the mystery game. Even when we were little, she'd always liked to riddle me silly riddles, to trick me with word play until I'd scream and chase her around the house.

She stood there silently, lips pressed together, as if daring me to guess.

"Don't be so tiresome," I said. "It's childish."

Her face reddened, and she slammed a hand down flat on the table. Mam and I both jumped, and I rescued a cup that'd been danced right close to the edge.

"You think you're the only one in this house, don't you?" She sniffed, swiped at her nose. "The only *woman*."

I think I must have gaped at her then, this pale stranger. Even her hair, always so thick and shining, looked lank, dull. It hung in strings in her face. She looked witchy, and I thought maybe it wasn't a good time to argue with her. Then I noticed something else: a whiff of sour coming across the table, a nasty smell off of her clothes. What in the world ailed her?

"Well, is it your, um, time of the month?" I said, trying to sound concerned, but not too know-it-all superior.

She laughed at that until she had to put a hand on the back of the chair to steady herself. "Oh, you wish," she gasped. Then she laid the other hand on her belly.

And I noticed finally how the material pulled tight there, puckering a little over her hipbones. She laid her other hand over the first, looked down, caressed her stomach.

And I knew.

"Oh no, Becca."

"It wasn't to hurt you, Annie," she said, but the words

came out too fast and jerky. They sounded rehearsed, like lines from a school play. "He said he's going to marry me." She looked so young, yet there was a strange dignity to her posture. She held herself differently.

"But you never, you're always here."

Of course, I was the one who was often gone. It had never occurred to me to wonder what might be going on at home, when I was out there on the water.

"I told him . . . last week, when he was here. He promised to make things right."

No one had been to the house the week before. The weather had been so bad I'd decided not to go out. The boats were pulled up, and I hadn't seen Nathan except on the one regular night he came to dinner. I'd been home every day. He was the only visitor we'd had.

I'd been worried until I saw him pull up, the water all gray chop and whitecaps beyond. He'd just waved off my concerns. "Ah, bit of a tickly bender. Not so bad."

I stood up then. Heard my chair crash over behind me. I glanced at Mam, who kept chewing slowly, though now she looked alarmed, her gaze darting between the two of us, then skittering away to the sugar bowl, the salt shaker.

I fisted my hands in front of me. "It's not. It wasn't Nathan," I said in a low voice.

Rebecca glared at me for a minute, then all the bravery on her face crumpled away. Fat, childish tears rolled down her cheeks, clear snot dripped from her nose; it always did when she bawled.

"It was," she said stubbornly. "It is."

Mam cried out suddenly, looking at us, "What's happened?"

"Your daughter. She's gone to Canaan," I said and left the table. Left them both.

*That afternoon I saw a dark smudge on the horizon, a front mov-*ing in from the west. I brought the boat in early. But the idea of being shut up inside the house with Mam's prattle and Becca's guilty looks was not bearable. I thought if I had something to do with my hands, I might be able to put off thinking of that terrible mess; Nathan and me and my sister. So I sat on the front stoop and worked at untangling and splicing and retying a net that had fouled on a sunken tree the week before. I was out of mending line and decided I'd just have to salvage what I could and make a temporary repair.

Who could tell if it was worth it, if it would hold.

Two chickens wandered over when they saw me sit down outside. They hung about, clucking and murmuring and eyeing me sideways, hoping for a handout. They only wanted me there to feed and look after them. Well, I didn't want their company either.

"Shoo," I said and hissed at them. They flapped and scooted a few paces off, beady eyes still fixed on me, clucking to each other like gossipy old women.

"I haven't planned my own dinner yet," I said loudly. "Begone, biddies, you know what's good for you."

They moved a few paces off and settled down to grumbling and pecking the weeds for bugs and grubs.

I had wanted distraction, but fixing net was second nature by now. It took no attention at all, so thoughts of my sister and Nathan together jabbed at me, sharp and pitiless as hungry herons' beaks. I ought to send her away, I thought. At least for a while. But we had no other kin. And then who would care for Mam while I was out in the boat?

Rebecca was sixteen, but I thought her still childish in many ways. And no matter what she'd done, she was my little sister, my same blood. I had to look out for her. Dad would have said so. And the reverend had so often preached about family duty, I could have recited those sermons from memory. I shook my head and picked harder at a big snarl in the middle of the net. Worried and plucked until my fingertips were raw meat. I managed to free one strand.

And when we told Nathan, mightn't he just go away? He had no ties, he could simply leave and find work elsewhere. I wondered if he would. Then I wondered if I even wanted him to stay. Perhaps there really was no Nathan, as I thought of him; perhaps I'd whipped him up out of the goods at hand. The way Rebecca stitched makeshift dresses to match what she saw in her magazines.

I winced and worked on. My fingers throbbed, and I was glad of it. The pain made it easier to concentrate on the job, at least for short spells. But I finally grew impatient. Mending the rips and tears seemed tedious, too small and precise.

And blame Rebecca as I might, who had really led her astray? I was the one who'd brought Nathan to the house, under cover of a lie. I had used him and let him use me, not even betrothed, in our house. With my mother and sister barely two rooms away.

I dropped the net in the dirt and rubbed my face. My eyes fairly twitched from staring so hard at all the tiny knots and splices. One of my fingers was rubbed raw and bleeding.

Maybe it was my fault. Maybe I had shown Rebecca what to want and how to go about it with Nathan or some other man. Of course it must be another man. Surely she was just frightened to say; perhaps the scoundrel was married already.

I picked up the net again and fingered the unraveling strands. I thought about cutting out the whole great snarl in the middle and splicing it anew. No one could expect to repair such damage with so little left to work with.

I bent my neck and tried my teeth on one edge of the ratted mess. No use.

"Damn it all to hell," I muttered. Then bunched the net in both hands and threw it away from me, hard. It thumped down in the yard, and the two nosy hens took off for the shed, trailing outraged squawks behind them.

I couldn't even fix a damned simple net. Much less all our stupid, stupid mistakes.

But Rebecca wouldn't tell me another name, no matter how I begged or threatened or pleaded. I wanted her to break down, admit it was some local waterman come sniffing around the house while I was out on the boat.

"Mayhap he already has a wife and thought he'd have you on the side, too," I snapped at her one morning.

She'd not said a word then, just gotten up from the table and gone to her room.

No matter how I buzzed and stung around her, she would not look at me or name names again, not even Nathan's. Nor the when and where, never mind the why of it.

Maybe we hadn't been to church in a while, but I knew very well what was expected of a family in this sort of trouble. Such things happened around these islands more than folks liked to let on. And if a bride seemed a bit thick-waisted at the altar, or her baby came earlier than the midwife predicted, people were usually inclined to be nearsighted and have short memories. It all hinged on doing what was expected and right. In this place, so small and isolated, everyone has to at least get along. For you never know when you'll desperately need the goodwill of your neighbors.

And I knew well enough what Dad would have expected. No, demanded.

The father must marry Rebecca. Whoever ruined her must be the man to make it good.

Above all, I refused to cry. I would first get hold of Nathan Combs and make him tell me what a lie it was. We expected him to dinner the next night, so I would wait for him down at the beach, catch him before he got to the house. I wanted him alone for this coming talk. Having decided that, I felt better.

I walked down to the pier around five and sat huddled against the wind on an upturned crate, Dad's old stained sou'wester wrapped around me. Already it was all but dark, though I could see as far as the Hog Island light, a globe of misted light to the north.

After a while, I don't know how long, his pale blue skiff ghosted toward me out of the scrappy fog.

He beached it and splashed out in high black rubber boots. Headed across the sand, whistling. He hadn't seen me yet, I was sure.

"Nathan," I said.

"Lord, but you give me a start," he said, swerving and coming toward me. He reached out, but I stood my ground, arms folded. But he seemed to take that as a new game, for he just advanced and wrapped me in a bear hug, growling playfully. I found it difficult not to go all soft then, but I managed to keep my back stiff and straight.

He finally let me go, stepped back, and tilted my chin up. He looked at last into my eyes. "What?"

"It's more like who," I said. "And when." Then I knew I would cry in a minute if I didn't get on with it. I'd meant to ask calmly, to wait for his astonished laugh, to hear him swear he certainly hadn't been the one.

But instead I said all in a rush, "Rebecca's having a baby. Why, why did you?"

"Hold on," he said, but I felt a cold fist turn in my stomach, for I could see even in the near dark that his face didn't look as surprised as I'd imagined it ought. "Why did I what?"

"I hate a liar, Nathan Combs. Think hard on that thing first. But liar or not, if you . . . if you're the one, then you have to do something about it."

He took a deep breath, let it out again slowly. "Your sister . . . I was with her, Annie, but just the once."

All the air went out of me in a gust. "When?" I snapped, as if I could prove him wrong with details.

"Two months? It was . . . October."

I recalled that back then at least one night he'd had to stay, the weather was so bad. After dinner he had met me outside, as I was coming back from the privy, and we'd slipped into the storeroom again.

Dear God, I thought. Was he going to tell me that after he had stood me up to face the window there, my sweating hands slipping on the sill as he gripped me from behind, that he had enough hunger left to go on to my sister as well? I shuddered at the pictures that flashed in my head of her white, white skin against his tan; her dark hair falling around his shoulders like a silky black curtain; his mouth pressing down hard on her soft red one.

"Annie." He stepped closer again and tried to steal an arm around me, but I knocked his hand away.

"Don't. Just tell it."

He drew a deep breath and rubbed a hand over his face. Well, I refused to believe it would hurt him to speak the words anything like it would hurt me to hear. But I had to hear, for I wanted to know how bad the damage and just how bitter I should feel.

"I went to sleep on the sofa," he said. "After you went to bed."

And then, just before dawn, it seemed someone had slipped under the quilt next to Nathan. He'd turned and felt warm bare skin.

"Hands on me, touching. Fingers against my lips, for quiet. And so . . . I thought it was you."

In spite of the aching empty pain in my chest, I snorted, then laughed out loud, the sound harsh in my ears.

"All right." He glanced at me, looked away. "After a while, I did know. But by then . . ."

The wind was picking up from the west. I crossed my arms against a chill gust from the water and shivered inside Dad's old oilskins.

I told you she wasn't in her right mind, I wanted to say. *Yet you took advantage.* I needed something hard and ugly to throw in his face, something to hurt him. But how could I say that? It was only part of a lie I had told.

He must have known I had made it all up, too, even before then. Yet he'd never said anything. I wondered if he would throw it up to me now.

"She came to me," he began again, slowly.

No. I wouldn't let him shift the blame to my sister. Even if I wanted to so badly myself.

"Oh, men are different, is that it?" I slammed a fist into his chest. He staggered back a step. "You can't be held responsible?" I hit him again, panting. "Can you dare stand there and tell me the rest?"

I didn't really want to hear any more. But if nothing else, he would not see me weaken. No, I was determined I would never forgive either one of them.

"My God, Annie. What else do you want? It's done."

"Yes, you saw to that."

"But is she sure?"

When he said that, he looked small to me. He looked, I don't know what—frightened, more like a boy.

"The girl's sick as a cat, pukes at every smell. Says she hasn't bled since . . . since then. Her dresses are getting tight in the waist. What more proof do you want me to bring out?"

I sat on the crate again and took a shuddering breath. "And she says you promised to marry her."

He looked truly stunned then. "But how . . . I didn't even know."

"Well, now you do."

"Annie, that's not . . . I can't."

Of course he couldn't, I didn't want him to. He was mine. I had wanted him.

I still did.

The wind howled again, bending the scrubby trees near the shoreline. The cold slap of it through the bare branches felt like judgment on us. The high whine of it was like Granny Jester's voice, speaking from the grave into my ears. *Selfish, selfish, selfish.*

"Whether you promised or not, you must do it, Nathan. That's what a man does when a girl he meddles with is caught short."

My parents had taught us that when you broke something, you had to take steps. Make it right. Mend or pay. Surely he knew that. It had occurred to me at least once, in the past months, that if I turned up in a family way, Nathan would do what was expected. I had already entertained that thought. So who was the meddler?

He looked away and jammed his hands into the pockets of his oilskin jacket. "And what if I say I won't do it?"

"I'll go to Cobb's. I'll tell the old man." In truth, I could not imagine ever doing this. But I stared at him, daring him to disbelieve me.

He stared back as if I'd lost my last ounce of sense, and didn't say anything for a minute. Then sighed, as if he gave up. "You're a cool one, Annie Revels. I don't know another woman who'd say such a thing."

So he had given in. I hadn't known I could be so strong, to bend a grown man to my will. There was precious little pleasure in it, I can tell you.

"I don't want to hear about any other goddamn women you might know," I said. "Now come into the house. You'll have to break the news to Mam. She likes you, God save her poor old soul."

We walked up side by side, not touching. Once, when I nearly slipped in the sand, he did put out a hand to me. But I pretended not to see, and it fell back against his side with the muffled sound of a dull slap.

When we came in, Rebecca, who'd been standing by the window, took one look at our faces and bolted to her room. I made her come back out and gripped her elbow to keep her there. I couldn't look at her face, I hated her so just then. So I looked away, out the window, and my sister stood by, trembling, as Nathan told Mam that he was come to ask for her daughter's hand.

Mam looked over at me. I felt chilled when I saw her pleased, innocent smile. No blame to her; she couldn't know. I closed my eyes and shook my head.

There was a short, dreadful silence.

Then Nathan said in a choked voice, "Since your husband is gone, I . . . talked to Annie, Mrs. Revels. But of course, I need your blessing, too."

Rebecca whimpered, and I tightened my grip. If I hadn't been holding her arm, I'd have run from the room myself.

"I'm asking for Rebecca," he said a bit louder. "For her hand."

Mam looked back at him and frowned. "Something wrong with that girl," she said querulously. "It's plain."

"Yes, ma'am. I'll look after her," he said, in a near whisper.

Mam looked over at me, hesitated, and finally nodded, but she still looked puzzled. "She'll not be such a handful as the elder, I suppose. Well now, Annie. Where's our dinner?"

We ate mostly in silence, except to ask for something out of reach. Once in a while Rebecca or Nathan would sneak a look down the table at me, though I noticed they avoided looking at each other. I almost wanted to laugh, but it would have turned to crying soon enough. No, I would be strong, like Dad. Not weak, like Mam. Not foolish, like Rebecca, nor false like Nathan.

Yet I had not been honest, either.

In some strange way, I thought I was still getting what I wanted. I'd wanted Nathan here; now he had to come and live with us. Not in the way I'd imagined, of course. I no longer had to keep him from Rebecca; it was too late for that. Somehow there seemed a slight, odd comfort in that, to know no more worry need be spent. Just that morning, I'd understood that if Nathan refused to marry my sister, he would have to go away from here forever, willingly or not. Perhaps we were isolated, but we had standards; we weren't animals.

I'd had a couple of days to think about just how badly I wanted him and what was the worst I could stand. I still wasn't sure. In the months we'd been meeting on the water and he had been coming to visit, he had never mentioned marriage to me.

That I still loved him, despite what he and Rebecca had done, had been the bitterest knowledge I'd ever gained. But there it was.

Besides, he'd never yet said that he loved me. He was thirty years old, he'd finally told me, had been in the Army, and neither before he'd come back from the war nor after, had he ever been married. Around here most wed young, the women at fourteen or fifteen sometimes, the men at eighteen. Twenty at the latest. After that, often as not, they stayed single. Most of the fellows who worked as guides for the Cobbs were single, and some of those weren't young, either. The kind of man who liked that work seemed to be the kind who stayed a bachelor all his days.

The bitterest thought of all was this: Why had it happened to my sister and not me? His milt had never rooted in my belly during all our times in those sea-rocked beds. In the six months or so since we'd been taking our pleasure with each other, I'd never missed a single monthly. Never even been late. I was regular as the damned calendar on the kitchen wall.

Now we would be under the same roof, but he would be married to Rebecca. Looking back now, I have to wonder what exactly I had expected of such a foolish arrangement. Of course I still wanted him. But I still believe that I never plotted, even in the darkest corner of my mind, to play it false. I never gloated and thought: *As soon as they are married, Nathan will be here with me. He will be mine.* I had already decided I would never touch him. Never be with him again, not in that way.

Nine

In the next few days, I did wonder if Nathan might run for it.
Rebecca avoided me in the house, keeping to her room unless she had to use the privy. Sending Mam out at mealtimes with some excuse: She was ill, she wasn't hungry. She didn't grow thin, though, so I assumed she was slipping into the kitchen at odd hours to eat.

But Nathan arrived for his wedding early on Christmas Eve day. The weather was fine, unseasonably warm for December. He didn't have to work, he said, because the few guests at the Cobb's Island Hotel this holiday seemed more interested in downing liquid cheer than in freezing their feet in an open boat waiting for a target to flap by. I wondered if he'd told the Cobbs he was getting married, but I wouldn't ask. Whenever I turned, it seemed he was looking at me with saddened eyes, as if someone had died. But I turned away quickly, still angry. Still afraid his gaze could weaken me.

We piled into Nathan's blue skiff, Mam bundled up like an Eskimo grandmother, and putted across to the mainland. In Wachapreague we interrupted the supper of a justice of the peace for a few minutes to have Rebecca and Nathan joined in marriage.

I'd worried some that if I went along, I wouldn't be able to stand it. And that if I didn't, either one or both of them would balk. But the disgruntled justice, who smelled of fried chicken and greens in his gravy-spotted undershirt; his fat, curious, staring wife; the hasty, mumbled reading of legal claptrap—it all had the feeling of buying a license or filing a deed. None of it undid me the way a real wedding with flowers and lace dresses and crying relatives might have. I felt untouched.

As we left the justice's house, we passed the Fox and Sons Funeral Home, where two men were unloading a limp body from the bed of a dray wagon. A weeping woman sat huddled in a shawl on the wagon box, staring at nothing. The dead man wore the sweater and oilskins of a waterman. I didn't know any of these folks, so we only nodded and went on. But Nathan took off his hat and stopped and spoke with them a moment.

"What happened?" I asked, when he turned back and caught up with us.

"Dragged overboard, got snarled in a net."

We stood looking after the body and its bearers as they entered the somberly painted building.

"He didn't belong to be out this time of year," I said, knowing my words were foolish, because it was oyster season, after all. But suddenly I wanted to turn away from us the bad luck and sorrow that seemed to radiate from that sad little scene.

I was surprised when Nathan said, "Maybe not." After a moment he added, "Though times, we all do what we oughtn't."

I looked at him sharply, but he was already turning away.

The Hotel Wachapreague was decorated for the holidays with fresh evergreen boughs and expensive fruit wreaths and red velvet bows, but their kitchen was shorthanded. The inedible lunch we were served actually raised my spirits. Each little mishap or disappointment of the day seemed to confirm that this was not really an occasion to celebrate, nor a true and binding thing, but an unpleasant business to be endured and forgotten.

The night that followed seemed much worse. We returned just before dark and ate a cold supper of sliced Virginia ham and stale biscuits with cider. Rebecca put Mam to bed, then the three of us sat uneasily around the table, drinking coffee. Talking little and looking up barely at all.

Finally, Rebecca set her cup in the saucer. "I've got gifts to wrap."

We had set up a tree halfheartedly the day before, a spindly mainland cedar with a few glass balls and paper stars tied on it. Mam was mighty pleased, though, and admired it for an hour at least.

Rebecca took her plate into the kitchen.

After she left, Nathan said quietly, "I'll stay here tonight, Annie. But tomorrow I'm going back to Cobb's."

That wasn't what I'd expected. I had already taken my things from the bedroom I had shared for over ten years with my sister. But even before that, I'd spent a whole day clearing out Granny's old room off the kitchen. I'd burnt the paper trash and boxes, had tossed out the most ancient preserves. Things I couldn't yet part with, I'd stacked or leaned against one wall. I suppose I could have been hard and insisted Nathan and Rebecca squeeze in there instead, though the pantry was obviously much too small for two. My generous act was more sham than anything; the most important thing was that I had memories of Nathan and me in there, that first night he'd come to dinner and other nights, after. I wouldn't give up that room and the recollections that went with it to anyone else.

So I'd fitted Granny Jester's old double bedstead back together and given it to Rebecca, then moved my single bed into the tiny room where Gran had died.

But Nathan knew none of my reasons, so he pushed away from the table and shook his head. "I've thought hard about this, Annie. Whether I should take Rebecca and leave the Shore altogether. Or go to Newport News, maybe to the shipyard."

I felt a prickle of panic. "Then there'll be no one home

to take care of Mam. I can't go out on the water and leave her alone. She'll wander off or burn the house down around her trying to light the stove. And we'll both starve if I don't go out in the boat."

"And I can't take Rebecca to Cobb's Island. I share a bare cottage with three other guides. Maybe I could get a loan from the old man, scrape up enough cash to build us a—"

"No need," I said quickly. I reached out, almost laid a hand on his arm before I realized and pulled back. "This place is big enough. And she'll need help after the—oh, with things."

"She could still look after your mother. If I did somehow take her to Cobb's."

"But you can't."

"I can't?" He shoved back from the table and glared at me. "So you'll arrange all our lives now, like the Almighty? The hell with that."

I'd never seen that expression on him before. As if, at least for the moment, he hated the sight of me. I wanted to shout back; I wanted him to stop staring at me with that terrible look on his face. This whole thing was not going the way I had hoped.

"I only meant—"

"We've ruined things bad enough. How in God's name can you want it to be this way? Me here, a baby underfoot. You can't mean for me to stay."

How could I explain when I could not justify my own feelings to myself? If I had answered, "I love you, Nathan. I think I may hate you, too. That's why you must marry my sister," I'd sound like a lunatic, crazier than my own Granny, unless we *both*—but my Methodist-trained mind clamped down hard on wherever that stray thought was leading.

So I only said, "What good is marrying Rebecca if you don't plan to be a husband or a father? If nothing else matters, Nathan, that child is yours." I looked away, hoping it wasn't clear in my eyes how little I had thought of the child, or yet cared.

"I thought you meant a marriage in name, to stop talk. To give the baby a father. But not here, in your house."

"Then stay at Cobb's, for a while. It will work out in the end." I believed it might, after a while. I was still angry at both of them. But I couldn't imagine cutting off my own nose, like the old saying. To not see Nathan at all seemed the cruelest possibility, then.

"You think so," he said doubtfully. He glanced away, as if looking for something or someone. Then looked back at me strangely.

"Annie," he said. This face he turned to me was the old Nathan again.

I looked away, down at the table. Anywhere else. "What."

"You know, don't you . . . that I did it because you asked. But suppose—"

Rebecca came back then, head down, a few packages in her arms. She set them carefully under the tree, then straightened, a hand at the small of her back. Already she had the mannerisms of a pregnant woman. Sometimes I'd come into a room and find her standing, eyes vacant, caressing her still-flat belly. If she saw me, she'd look stricken and turn away, pretending to straighten her dress.

But the last few days, the sight hadn't affected me the same way. I didn't care as much. It wasn't a baby I had wanted so badly. I'd never even imagined myself growing big that way or rocking a child in my arms. Being responsible for my sister and my mother had been more than enough for me.

Rebecca fiddled with the tree ornaments and tidied the table. She glanced at Nathan a few times, then sighed and said she was tired. She went off to bed.

He turned to me again. "Suppose—just suppose—that I asked you to go off with me, right now."

I clenched my hands in my lap, under the table, to keep them there. A terrible pain was growing in my chest. It felt like an answer coming, a wicked, selfish one. But I shook my head.

"Wait. Don't say no yet."

He leaned across the table toward me, and I could barely keep myself from reaching out to touch him.

"I could send money," he said. "You see? Make sure they had what they needed. The child, too."

I wanted to agree. Why not, as long as Mam and Rebecca were provided for? And this nameless baby I couldn't begin to picture. But I had taken on the responsibility for my family; it would still be abandoning them. The sort of thing people gossiped on in these parts, a black betrayal to make them cluck tongues and shake heads. The wrongness and shame would stay with me, would cling to us like a black shroud, no matter where we went. It would go on and on; it would mean making up new lies.

"No. No, we can't."

But oh, how I wished we could.

I went off to my own bed then. And for aught I know, Nathan sat up all night in that chair and never went to sleep at all. I preferred to think it might be so.

It felt so strange the next morning; Nathan and Rebecca and I at the breakfast table. I fussed extra long over Mam's oatmeal so I wouldn't have to look at them. Of course he was right. How could we do this day after day? But I was stubborn, determined to make it work somehow.

Rebecca seemed more relaxed, and I hated to see the way she smiled at Nathan. But I had insisted on this, had made it possible. So I bit back any hard words that came to me and passed the salt and the sugar, and we ate. Then I took our coffee and a plate of ginger cookies into the parlor, and told everyone to come sit around the tree.

In years past, Dad had played Santa and handed out gifts. So I hesitated, thinking how to arrange things now.

As I pondered it, Rebecca said to Nathan, "Here, hand

out Mam's package first, then Annie's. Then mine." As if he had always been part of our custom.

I stared at her. How had she known what I had wanted? I didn't like it much that she'd said it first.

Nathan hesitated. Then he got up, fumbled with boxes and tissued-wrapped parcels and read the tags. Then he handed things around silently. We opened our packages and tried to sound pleased with what we'd gotten. Mam enjoyed herself, at least. Nathan had brought her a box of chocolate-covered cherries, the kind you have to go to the mainland to buy. He gave Rebecca a bolt of nice blue woolen material to make a new maternity dress. I hadn't gotten a gift for him, but he handed me a flat square wrapped with shiny red paper. Inside, from under pat-terned tissue paper, I pulled out a cream-colored slip with lace trim.

I lowered it quickly to my lap, folded the soft stuff over and over until it was a fat silk square. "Thank you," I said stiffly.

"I hope it's all right," he said in a low voice. "I got it a while back."

"How pretty. I'm sure it'll fit," said Rebecca. Her voice sounded too cheerful. I nodded but didn't want to see if the look in her eyes matched the tone of her voice.

I went on and opened my next gift, a pair of knitted blue mittens and a wool scarf from Rebecca. I gave out my gifts to her and to Mam, hairpins and combs and a hand mirror painted on the back with roses. Then I got up and left, to check on the roasting duck, I said. But then I slipped into my room after I'd basted the bird and held the slip in front of me before a cracked mirror I'd dragged out from the corner. I sniffed the store-newness of it and rubbed the silky material across one cheek.

My tanned skin looked different with that slip against it; the creamy off-white was just right. I held the slip with one hand, then pushed my hair all on top of my head with the other. I sniffed the silk. It looked and felt clean and new, like the nice shop it had certainly come from. Nathan must have gone all the way to Cape Charles to find it.

A while ago, he'd said. He must have meant before the night I'd waited for him on the pier. Who would have guessed he'd be the kind to think of a beautiful present weeks before Christmas? So perhaps I'd slighted him in other ways, but I wouldn't think of that now. It was what he'd chosen to give me that I marveled at. The kind of gift a man bought for a woman he thought was beautiful.

Nathan went back to Cobb's that afternoon, as he'd said he would. He did promise Rebecca he'd be back sometime soon. "Often as I can, anyway."

Then our family fell back into our old winter routines. Rebecca sewed all day, though now she made baby things instead of dresses. One day I was surprised to see Mam working away with her big wooden hook at a pink and blue woolen square. Crocheting was a task she hadn't attempted in years, but when I asked, she said she was making a crib blanket. True, it was coming out lopsided, but no baby would notice that.

I mended net and spliced line and polished brass during the day. I reread the few books we had lying about. And I took over baking the bread, and most evenings, I cooked our dinner.

For a slender girl, Rebecca grew an astonishing belly. After her first few months, the sickness passed, and she was ravenous all the time. I came upon her all hours of the day, eating crusts of bread, handfuls of walnuts, a dripping spoon of honey straight from the jar. Once I came into the kitchen before dinner and caught her gnawing furtively at a slice of raw meat. Her arms and legs stayed thin, but her face bloated until she looked like a different person by her sixth month. Older, worn, and disappointed somehow. She tired easily heaving all that bulk around, and her breath came in gasps. She complained she could never get to sleep. Lines grew at the corners of her mouth, and bluish shadows under her eyes.

Nathan visited rarely, though he did come for a few hours at least every other week. When he was there, I went to my room early, so I wouldn't have to watch them get up at the end of the evening and walk to the room they shared. If Rebecca so much as yawned during dinner, I made sure to go to bed after the pie. While I was awake, the thought of them together in Granny's old bed was awful. Still, I couldn't stop myself from imagining what it might be like and got no sleep either.

I turned in early those nights and stayed in bed as late as I could. I tried to sleep more and more. In my dreams, sometimes, I still met Nathan alone, and then for a while he was mine.

When the weather turned to spring, and the water warmed, it would be time to take the dredge boat off the blocks. I wondered what mornings would be like, the times he came and stayed, then. We'd be leaving early, almost together, taking our separate boats out. Surely that would be strange.

I began to look forward to it.

Nathan came to help get the trawler back in shape for the water, though I hadn't asked. But I didn't turn the help down. First we sanded the bottom until we both ran with sweat. Then painted it, working side by side but not speaking except when we had to.

When we were almost done, the brush slipped from my hand. I grabbed for it desperately, but it squirted off in all directions like a small greased animal. It finally landed in the dirt and I cursed a blue streak; the copper bottom paint had splashed everywhere.

When I bent over to pick it up, Nathan was laughing.

"Look at you," he said, gasping for the breath to speak again.

I was spattered from head to foot. I felt paint running down my face, dripping from the ends of my hair, and finally I had to laugh, too. But then he leaned closer, maybe only to thumb a smear off the end of my nose. Like our first meeting out on the water, only then I'd been all-over mud and grease. But he stopped short, and I turned and walked back to the house to wash up. I stopped in the toolshed first, though, leaned against the wall, and cried for the first time in months. Then I wiped my nose, got out the mineral spirits, cleaned the brush and myself, and went back out to finish the job.

That spring and summer I knew it was likely I'd see him out on the water sometimes, but at least it would be at a distance. And if it hurt to think he was there, but not waiting for me, then I could pretend I was mistaken. Under those silly billed hats most of the Cobb's guides looked pretty much alike, anyhow, from a distance.

Maybe during those months he wanted to cross my path but tried not to. Nathan was a man with faults, but I knew now he could be thoughtful, too. I tried to look at my situation in this way: I hadn't expected to marry. I'd had no suitors; no one had ever come to Yaupon Island courting me. I hadn't given up anything when I met him except my maidenhood, which I'd never seen or touched and to be truthful hadn't really missed—a thing that, as far as I could tell, hadn't done me much good or been of any particular use. In return I'd gotten pleasure I hadn't even imagined existed. But now, I told myself, I'd have to be satisfied with my hand in the dark again and whatever dreams came afterward.

What I wouldn't—no, *couldn't*—do was dwell on what might be happening in the other room, at night after the quiet suppers, the days he came to visit.

One night in March when he'd stayed, I went to bed early as usual but couldn't sleep. So after a while I grabbed a shawl, and slipped boots on, and went out to walk around. For early in the year it was a bit warmer than usual, with no insects out yet to attack in humming swarms the way they did in summer. The moon shone bright, though it was thin as a nail paring, but the sky was clear and there were stars aplenty. I took a turn around the whole sleeping island, listening to crickets and the slosh of the tide until I felt more inclined to go on back to bed.

Returning toward the back side of the house, I saw the faint glow of the lamp I'd left burning in my room to the left. To the right, three darkened squares of window: the kitchen, Mam's room, and Rebecca's. Too hard to think of it as Nathan's, too. As *theirs*. I knew he was inside it at that moment, though, lying beside my sister. I went straight for the kitchen door, but then after a few steps I veered right. Came right up to their window. It was shoved open a few inches, but the inside of the room was dark. I can't say what I hoped to hear or see, but I stayed, a hand braced against the rough boards of the house to steady myself as I stood in the sand and weeds, not moving.

After a while I heard a faint rustle, a scrape and creaking

of springs, as if someone had turned over in bed. Next a long, drawn-out breath or a sigh. Then silence. Perhaps these weren't actually sounds of pleasure or of anything but what you'd expect to hear from a room where two people merely slept. But I backed away, a hand over my mouth, and nearly tripped over the hem of my nightgown. Then I ran all the way back to my side of the house.

In my room, I lay on my back again on the narrow rope bed. The sheets were clean and smooth and smelled of fresh air and soap. The mattress was comfortable enough. I turned on my side, then on my back again, and touched myself in the old way through the thin cotton of my nightgown. But I felt no pleasure in the press of my own fingers on my own flesh. I let my arm fall back to my side again and didn't get up to douse the light. I left it burning all night. And did not sleep.

The June night Rebecca went into labor was hot enough to melt a brass monkey. It had rained all day; so it felt even hotter, downright steamy indoors. We'd put Mam to bed with one of her headaches, and I had stripped to my camisole, bare feet, and a thin, worn pair of Dad's old britches to do the dishes. I'd pinned up my hair but still sweat trickled down my back, and the lone mosquito that kept buzzing my ears would not come within slapping range. Time to mend the screens again, I thought, racking up the clean dishes almost hard enough to break them.

Rebecca paced the house from one end to the other, walking, walking, till it made me tired just to watch. She'd complained steadily all day of various ailments, her constant stream of words making a list of grievances I could all but see hanging in the air before us.

She was going to be sick from the heat.

Her back hurt.

Her feet were swollen.

She couldn't sleep.

She had gas.

She couldn't eat a bite.

No one cared if she died of misery.

I nodded to them all and said little. Finally, I finished the dishes and went to lie on the sofa, feeling hotter and sweating even harder, if that were possible. I was tired and sunburned from a long day crabbing. I'd had to weed the garden when I got in since Rebecca could no longer bend around the huge obstacle that was her middle. Usually, I tried to listen to her complaints patiently; it took too much energy to argue in such weather. And she was clearly so miserable I did truly feel sorry for her.

She stopped in front of me for a moment. "Did you hear what I said, Annie?"

"Yes. And you're wrong. I don't want you to suffer, Becca."

She looked skeptical but finally sat, though, and quieted down, and fanned herself some more with a folded newspaper.

It was true; as angry as I'd been at her and at Nathan, I would never have wished her all this discomfort. I'd overheard talk between women gossiping at the general store, or after church over cookies and lemonade, or on the street; I'd gathered that having a baby was a tiring, painful, lengthy business and terribly hard on the mother. I had vague recollections of Mam's illnesses, but those had come after Rebecca was born. I wasn't experienced in such matters otherwise; but I didn't see how childbirth itself could be too much worse than this.

After a half hour, Rebecca was up again and pacing, lumbering around and groaning like a gut-shot bear. Shooting me reproachful looks as I tried again to explain that what she saw as my lack of sympathy was just plain exhaustion.

"*You're* exhausted," she snapped. "Try hauling all this weight around. It kicks and jabs and pokes my ribs. I can't get a minute of sleep. Annie Revels, you just have no idea."

That was true. But then I thought: *No, and thanks to you, I suppose I never will.* I knew that was unfair, of course. It had taken the two of them, not just Rebecca.

But at least she sat again, and I hoped the pacing was at an end.

"I wonder if I might die," she said suddenly. "If I did, you'd be relieved. Why, maybe you'd even be happy." She heaved herself up out of the chair again.

At this point I think I did begin to feel mean, and so I had just opened my mouth to say, *Then have pity. Go ahead and die and get it over with.* But then a blank, shocked expression smoothed out the angry, spiteful lines that had creased my sister's face a moment before.

"Something just *popped*." She gave me a look of pure horror.

And before I could sigh or laugh or shake my head, a gush of water ran down her shaking legs and all over the floor.

"Mother of God," I said, sitting up. "What's that?"

I remembered Mrs. Killmon, the midwife, had said, "Be sure to send for me right away around when she's due. Don't wait till her water breaks." It took a good long while to get from one island to the next, and if it was flat calm out there, I'd have the devil of a time getting to Hog Island and back in any good time.

"Oh no." Rebecca started to cry. "It's coming, isn't it?"

"Well, I'd think you'd be glad," I snapped, because I was suddenly afraid, too. It seemed early yet; Mrs. Killmon had not expected her to deliver for another two weeks or so. I rushed over to the hall pegs and yanked down my oilskins.

"Why, just think, honey," I said, trying to keep my voice steady. "This is a good thing, Becca. Soon you can stop being so big and miserable."

"Oh, but it hurts. Just now I felt an awful, awful pain." She staggered over to Dad's old chair and sat down. "Annie, I need a towel. Where are you going?" Her eyes looked glazed over, like a snared rabbit's.

I ran to get the towel first. "Why don't you lie down on

the bed?" I wiped her cold, sweating face with one corner, then handed the towel to her.

"I don't want to," she cried, doubling over, clutching her belly again. It must have been my imagination, but I thought for a moment I saw the taut calico fabric stretched over her middle ripple as this contraction took her.

She gasped, and I hovered but couldn't think of anything very useful. "Rebecca, how long since the one before?"

She shook her head, panting. Damp hair stuck to her flushed cheeks. "I don't know."

"Well, I'm going for Missus Killmon now."

She tried to struggle up again. "Take me with you."

She stared at me, holding my gaze like a drowning person. I couldn't get up and go, I couldn't even look away. My sister in her pain had one of my hands in a death grip between both of hers, as if I were God and could save her. So I knelt next to the chair and stroked her arm. "Becca, be reasonable. I have to get her so she can help you, make sure it all goes right. I'd take you in the boat, but we can't leave Mam alone. And it's not that far. You've just started. It takes a long time to have a baby."

"Oh, I suppose you're the expert on that," she said, then looked stricken. "Dear Lord, I didn't mean that." She grabbed my hand.

"I have to go." I was beginning to feel as panicked as she looked. What if . . . "Of course you're afraid," I said. "Why, I'll bet everyone is at such a time. But . . . but it's normal. You'll be fine."

"But I did it on purpose. Now I'm going to *die*." She squeezed her eyes shut. Tears rolled out from under her clenched lids.

"What?" I tried to pull one sweating hand away. Her pale, thin fingers were iron clamps, crushing mine. I felt like I'd been hooked on a line. "What do you mean?"

"Annie, Annie." Her voice rose higher, babbling. "I didn't so much want to hurt you. But I was tired of being the one to stay home, change Mam's sheets. Never go anywhere. You at least got to see folks sometimes."

"Oh, surely. I've had a ball out there with the crabs and eels." I pried her clutching fingers up, one at a time, and saw she'd dug her nails into my skin; the little crescent gouges were red with blood. "Now listen, Becca—"

But she wouldn't. "When I saw him that first night, I wanted him to notice me. But he only laughed. He treated me like . . . like I was *simple*. And I was so put out when you sent me off to get Mam to bed. So after I did, I came right back. But . . . no one around."

She gasped; another pain contorted her face. "I looked for you two all over. Even outside. And at last I saw . . . through the window."

That night, looking over Nathan's shoulder, when I'd thought for a moment there was something in the moonlight, a pale face shape outside Granny's room, I had been right.

"I only thought I might have what you did," she said.

"Why not? No one ever comes. Who will I meet here? But now Nathan doesn't want me like—"

"I don't want to hear," I said through gritted teeth. "Stop it."

"He won't even touch me."

I managed to snatch my other hand back at last. And though I hadn't actually thought of doing it, I slapped her face. "Stop it," I said. "You just be quiet."

She held a hand over the red mark on her cheek and sobbed. She stared at me after that as if I was a stranger who'd wandered in.

I knelt in front of her again and patted her knee. Took up one of her hands and kissed the back of it, the way she had done with mine when we were little. "I'm sorry," I said, trying to speak softly, afraid if I let myself shout it would overwhelm me, that rage and betrayal, and I might hit her again. Knock her clean across the room.

She nodded silently. Her eyes were wide, staring.

"Now I'm going to take the skiff," I said slowly, "And get Missus Killmon. I want you to go lie down on the bed in your room. Why don't you take off those wet things?"

She nodded again, and a single tear trickled down her cheek.

You're a monster, Annie Revels. Unnatural. A monster.

That was how I felt, looking at my sister, barely more than a child and in the clutches of a woman's pain. For I could not forget what she had said: *He won't touch me.*

I could not stop thinking of that and exulting in it.

I helped her unbutton the top of her dress. Her small breasts looked swollen, the nipples showed as dark brown shadows beneath the thin, white cloth of her chemise. She stood, and I steered her into the bedroom. I hadn't set foot inside there since the wedding and didn't want to be there then. She walked so slowly I wanted to close my eyes and shove her on toward the bed, but I made myself walk even slower instead. I pulled a clean cotton nightgown over her head and helped her slide onto the mattress.

I don't know what I expected to see in there. The ghost of Nathan, who was very much alive? Or perhaps some evidence that, no matter what she'd just tried to tell me, he felt for Rebecca the same things he had for me. But the room was near about bare. There was not a thing to show that Nathan had ever set foot in it. Only her clothes on some pegs, a washstand, and Granny Jester's bed, the one she'd died in, raving. And Rebecca's old doll, the one Dad had carved, its wooden skin darkened with the years, lying beside her on the other pillow like some awful shrunken bridegroom.

"I'll be back in a little while, Becca. Don't worry."

I checked on Mam, who was still sound asleep. Then ran out of there. The moon was out, the water was calm, but I couldn't make the skiff go fast enough.

I lifted a hand from the tiller and wiped my eyes with the scratchy cuff of my oilskin jacket. I steered out into the channel, found the Hog Island light, a larger star in the northeast, and followed it.

Shortly I'd be passing the west side of Cobb's Island. But there was no time to make for its south shore, stop and try to find Nathan, to tell him he was about to have a baby. I didn't want to, anyway. Didn't want to see him at all at that moment because what my sister had told me changed nothing. He had known what he was doing after she'd slipped under that quilt. He'd just wanted what he wanted, right then.

Like all of us. I understood that much.

The weather turned a bit rough by the time I reached Hog Island. But I was glad of it, for that rising wind meant a faster sail back to Yaupon. I tied up, ran up the marl lane to Mrs. Killmon's cottage, and pounded on her door.

What I recall most of the ride back is the midwife clinging to her black leather bag with one hand and the gunwale with the other, a calico hat tied down tight over her pin curls. She was thrown about as I tacked wildly to take advantage of each gust. At one point, the freshening wind even took her bonnet, but she flapped a hand at me to never mind.

"Go on then, maid. I'll stitch up a new one bimeby."

I shouted out my worries as I steered: My sister was in terrible pain. She was young, not even seventeen yet.

Mrs. Killmon laughed at that. "Right many younger make mothers 'round here," she said. In the light of the swinging moon, I saw her smile kindly at me. "Of course, everyone is different. Don't you worry, though."

We arrived to find Mam still asleep and Rebecca standing, clutching the bedpost, moaning now that she just wanted to die.

Mrs. Killmon tsked at that and got her back on the bed. She sent me to get hot water and towels. I brought them back just as Rebecca was taken with a hard contraction and her scream chilled me, bones and blood. The midwife took one look at my face and sent me out again.

"Can't do my work properly if I have to worry about bystanders," she said and shut the door.

So my education in childbearing seemed destined to go no further than the gossip I already knew. I went back to the sofa but sat there tense as a bird dog on point, waiting news. For what seemed hours, though, all I heard was the steady murmur of the midwife's talking and humming, interrupted by an occasional scream or plea for heavenly deliverance from my sister.

What all was happening in there sounded terrible. I wished for company, someone to tell me it wasn't really that strange, that these things were natural, only to be expected. I even considered, and then again rejected, going for Nathan.

At last Mrs. Killmon cracked the door and ordered more water, clean rags, and handed me a pair of scissors. "Boil the devil out of 'em," she said briskly and slammed the door in my face again.

So I finally understood my part in this was simply to do what I was told, when I was told, and that was all. It was comforting to know that much, at least.

Still, I grew anxious as time passed and it seemed nothing had changed. At last I got up my nerve and knocked timidly on the door of my old bedroom.

"Is she all right?" I asked, trying to see through the doorway around Mrs. Killmon's bulk. On the bed, Rebecca raised her head. Her hair was matted with sweat, her fists clamped around towels the midwife had tied to the bedposts.

"No, I am not," she cried. "I'm dying."

"Doing very well," said Mrs. Killmon, who sat down again at the foot of the bed and began calmly knitting.

So I returned to my perch on the sofa. Then I paced. At last I came back and knocked again.

"Come in," shouted the midwife's voice, a bit sharper this time. I was just in the nick to see my sister raise herself on her elbows, panting and blowing, her legs spread well apart. Mrs. Killmon was bent over between Rebecca's knees, her hands busy. I smelled something—heated copper, the warm salt of blood.

"Sweet oil massage," she said. "Helps keep the mother from tearing . . . ah, that's good. Push now, honey child."

Rebecca made a terrible, twisted face, then barked out a harsh, strangled yelp. I was very grateful at that moment to be single and childless.

"There we are," said Mrs. Killmon, as she slipped her

hands under a greenish blue bundle that squeezed out all in a rush. Becca fell back limp, her eyes closed, face white as the pillows behind her.

I rushed over, terrified my only sister had just then died. But she seemed to be breathing fine. "Oh my, that's better," she said after a moment, and opened her eyes again. They looked bloodshot, exhausted, but relieved, too. "Which is it?"

"I can't see," I said. From where I stood, the baby's head seemed colored an alarming shade of blue green. It also looked terribly misshapen, pointed as a nun buoy.

My Lord, I thought. It's disfigured. The poor little thing's not right at all. I leaned over and whispered my fears to the midwife. I didn't want to alarm Rebecca.

Mrs. Killmon laughed and laughed. "Oh, they all look a sight, at first," she said, wiping the squalling infant down with clean rags and water. "It's a boy, honey," she called to Rebecca, as she deftly wrapped him in a clean towel.

Then she leaned closer to me and said low and confidential, "Oh, they heads all look squashed at first. Yours would, too, honey, after somebody pushed you right through a knothole."

He surely sounded healthy enough, squalling like a cat shut in a door. The midwife held out the scissors and asked if I wanted to cut the cord.

I looked down at what seemed to be a pale twisty rope lying on the rubber sheet, pulsing like a snake. I swallowed back a funny taste in my throat.

"No. No, thank you."

"Fine, then I'll do it. Here." She shoved the baby at me, then tied and snipped. I swallowed again and looked away, holding the squirming, sticky infant stiffly in front of me.

"There now," she said. "Take him in the kitchen and clean him up good. Then bring him back to his mother."

I carried Nathan's son to the kitchen sink for his first proper bath. He made mewling kitten sounds and snuffled against the cotton blanket and I was mortally sure I was going to drop him, but somehow we made it. He certainly looked nothing like the baby in the Carnation advertisement. He smelled of strangeness: wet salt, metal, the sulfur of marsh water. Some sort of goop covered his skin, cheesy white, despite Mrs. Killmon's brisk cleaning efforts. I tucked him securely under one arm, like a pocketbook, and pumped a couple inches of water in the sink. Added a trickle from the kettle till the bath felt lukewarm. Then I laid him in the water carefully.

I rubbed his stomach gently with a soft dishcloth. He set up a real howl then.

"Do all men hate to bathe right from birth?" I muttered.

His waving fist caught hold of one of my fingers. I stopped rubbing and peered down at him. Could he see me? It seemed his dark blue gaze looked right into me. I tried to find Nathan in him somewhere, but except for the thick shock of black hair that topped his head, I couldn't connect them at all. Nathan was handsome, green-eyed, and had a good, even smile. This baby sported a squashed muzzle and squinty blue eyes, but perhaps these features would improve with time. He also had what seemed to me a remarkably swollen set of balls, much too big for the rest of him.

"I know, it's all so strange," I said, as I wrapped him in a clean dish towel. "But I'm your aunt Annie."

He gave a wide yawn, and I had to smile. *That's right*, I thought. *Don't be impressed by family connections.*

Mam wandered into the kitchen then, and I thought at first to send her back to bed, until I saw through the window it was nearly light outside. Then I realized.

"Look, Mam. You've got your first grandchild."

She shuffled over and smiled down at the baby. Touched a finger to his cheek, and he turned his head, pursing his lips at the air.

"He's no fool. Got the Revels appetite," she said. Then, querulously, "And where's yours, maid? I'm an old woman, now."

I couldn't answer for a moment. *I'm the selfish daughter*, I almost reminded her. *The one sent to give you grief, remember?*

Instead I said, "Go sit down, Mam." It would do no one any good to take her addled words too much to heart. "In a bit, I'll have your oatmeal."

I finished drying the baby and took him back to the bedroom. Rebecca seemed to be asleep, but the midwife propped the baby in her arms anyway and pushed her nightgown aside to uncover one swollen breast. My sister mumbled and turned her head, but the baby only lay there quietly. Mrs. Killmon frowned. She tickled his mouth with her fingertip, and she guided his head until he got the idea and latched on to the nipple.

"Well, now. He's getting the hang of it," she said, putting scissors and other tools back into her bag. "You go on and get some sleep, honey. I'll sit up with them a while. I have to fill out the certificate. What's the name going to be?"

For the first time I realized I'd never heard either Rebecca or Nathan discuss what they'd call the baby, girl or boy. I hadn't thought about it. But then, he wasn't my baby.

"He doesn't have one yet," I said.

"I know that," she said patiently. "Well, never mind. I'll ask the mother when she's awake. Or will the father be in soon?"

I looked away and fiddled with the bedcovers, tucking and smoothing them in places they didn't need it. "He's off . . . at work. Someone would have to go get him."

Missus Killmon nodded. "Fine, then. You do that, dear. We'll be here."

She sat in the extra chair I'd dragged in from the dining table, took out her knitting, and began to hum, clacking away at a ball of red worsted.

I closed the door behind me and leaned back against it. Possible excuses went through my head, none I wanted to admit to out loud. I stood on one foot, then the other, but couldn't think of any way out. It was dawn, and I had no good reason not to take the boat to Cobb's Island and tell Nathan the news.

So I fed Mam, dressed her, and set out.

This time, the water was calm, and that was a relief. We all had been through enough this night, and I, like Rebecca, wanted only to rest. As I rounded the south point of Cobb's, I saw the long pier, which jutted out over the marsh grass from the sloping shell path that led to the hotel. I aimed for it, then squinted up at the rambling wooden structure. No one seemed to be stirring, but then it was early yet.

Off to the side stood a smokehouse, some sheds, and other outbuildings, among them the small whitewashed guides' cottages. Nathan would still be sleeping in one of them. Which was his? He had pointed it out to me once, from the water. Now they all seemed alike.

As I pulled up to the pier, an old man in denim overalls and a grease-stained shirt came out of the boathouse, sipping from a battered tin mug. He stood at the end of the pier and watched me approach, then set his mug down and caught my line when I tossed it up.

"You know Nathan Combs?" I asked. "Can you take him a message?"

He nodded.

I found an old crab-buy receipt in my oilskin pocket, and

with a pencil stub I'd once jammed into the mainsheet
block as a makeshift repair, I scrawled

BABY BOY NEEDS NAME.

I didn't sign it. Just folded the paper in half, wrote "N.
Combs" on the front, and handed it to the man.

"Got coffee," he said, jerking his head toward the boathouse. I thanked him but said no, and came about to head
back home. I'd never been on Cobb's Island yet, and that
morning I vowed, as I headed off, that I saw no reason to
set foot there in my life, ever.

Ten

Nathan came around noon. "Had to trade off some hunters from Philadelphia," he said. "We're shorthanded."

I nodded, opened the door wider, and stepped back. He pulled off his guide cap and came inside. "You're looking fine," he said. "How's Rebecca doing?"

I shrugged and folded my arms. "Seems all right. So does the baby," I said.

Nathan looked fine, too; still tanned and fit. But his cheekbones seemed sharper, closer to the surface, and his hair needed cutting. And after he had glanced at me once, he looked away and didn't meet my gaze again.

I led him to the room, his and Rebecca's. She was propped up in bed, nursing the baby. I went only as far as the door, then turned away. But not before I saw the pride on her exhausted face as Nathan came closer to take a look at his son. I left quickly then. I couldn't bear to hear a word.

They named the baby George, after his grandfather, and Nathan, after his father. My sister recovered quickly from her lying-in time and soon was insisting the child be baptized right away.

"What's the hurry?" I thought maybe she feared the baby might die somehow, as our little brother had. "He's healthy enough, Becca."

Or perhaps, I thought, she had gone near crazy being in the house, confined first by sickness and her girth, then by the demands of the baby, who nursed constantly. He was calm, though, and didn't cry much. Or maybe it was the lure of fashion, for Rebecca set to work at once on a new dress, claiming she couldn't squeeze into any of her old ones.

In any case, Nathan arranged little George's baptism to be done at Broadwater Methodist on Hog Island the following Sunday. We hadn't really attended there for years, not since before Dad died. But Nathan knew the new minister, Reverend Scarborough, who came by the hotel sometimes to hunt black duck and fish. Old Man Cobb gave him special rates, apparently.

I'd never asked a minister over to Yaupon, not even when we'd buried Dad. I thought the chief who'd helped us had said a nice short service over his casket. I suppose, looking back, I should have had a real reverend. But I don't think Dad, who was a Christian but hated enforced pew-sitting, would have cared much either way. Still, I allowed that a new baby ought to start out with all the advantages, so I agreed about the baptism. When I realized Rebecca expected me to come along, though, I hesitated.

"Oh, please, Annie. I can't hold the baby and watch Mam besides. And all the family should be there. Now that Dad's gone—please?"

"All right," I said finally, to get some peace. "All right."

We set out early the next Sunday. Nathan came in the blue skiff to carry us there.

"Well, ain't no wind, but it's a fair wind," he said as he cast off.

And he was right. We arrived in good time, nearly a half hour before the service. Rebecca and I had rarely been to the island since we'd attended school years back. But most of it was still as I recalled.

A fat cow and several skinny, skittish hogs roamed free on the beach and along the shell-paved streets. All the houses were yet whitewashed and well kept; clean laundry weighed down every clothesline I saw. The place had seen a few small changes, though. A block or so from the church was a new square-dance place. *The Red Onion*, read its fancy-painted sign, though it looked like any old barn to me. The Tillet General Store's canted porch and rusted tin roof appeared the same as when I had been ten and liked to buy a chunk of cheddar and pickles for my lunch there. I had fed Rebecca her first dill pickle at Tillet's counter, then laughed myself silly at the puckery face she'd made.

The store's sign still hung slightly crooked, its paint peeling no more and no less than seven years ago. But there were also two new-looking motor cars parked out front, alongside a small ox cart and a mule and wagon.

Down Main Street was the church, next to our old one-room school. We entered and sat, and right away I recalled the hardness of the pews, their backs so upright I'd always felt as if I had to lean forward. But then, Methodists don't come to church to get comfortable. So I sat straight as I could in the growing summer heat, taking in the plain wood altar, the fine but faded purple altar cloth, and the Sunday smells of hair pomade, flowery cologne, and sweat. I tried to stir the air a little with the cardboard fan the usher had handed me. But between the hard pew and the stuffy heat, soon I felt sticky and damp. My back gradually seized and stiffened like a wet shirt in a winter breeze.

I felt uneasy, too, wondering if folks were looking, taking their measure of us. We knew few people who might claim any firsthand knowledge of our doings these days, but gossip traveled from island to mainland and back, and no one ever bothered to keep track of how close to the original truth it was by the second or third retelling.

So perhaps we did raise an eyebrow or two or cause some whispers. Why not? It had to be rare Hog Islanders saw new people, save the few tourists who wandered over from Cobb's. And a few folks who'd come to play on a holiday trip wouldn't likely turn up in church of a Sunday.

The processional tapered off and the lessons commenced. I'd assumed we would be bringing little George Nathan up front to the baptismal font after the regular service was over. But right after the lay reader, a very tall, white-haired man in a black suit and vest, finished an epistle from Paul to the Romans, the minister asked the congregation to turn to the baptism service in their prayer books. Then he smiled and motioned at us to come on up.

I held the baby while Nathan helped Rebecca struggle up from her seat. She still looked a bit thick in the middle and must have been sore, for she moved clumsily. At the end of the pew she leaned over and said, "Give him to me," as if I had said I was going to keep the child.

So I handed her little George and she went on up the aisle. I slid out next, and waited while Nathan helped Mam. Then I took her frail, bony elbow, and we followed him to the front. I kept my gaze straight ahead. Mam was trembling; I could feel it all through her bones. But that was nothing new and probably meant little. She was right shaky even at home. As we approached the front, though it seems silly now, I felt the strange faces on either side knew all about the three of us, Nathan and Rebecca and I, and were passing judgment.

We stood around the chipped marble font and watched the minister for cues. Little George had slept through the hymns and prayers and kneeling, but now he was stirring, his mouth pooched like a bud, working as if he'd tasted something bad in a dream. Reverend Scarborough introduced himself, and though he looked a nice enough man,

I found myself wishing old Reverend Pennewell was still there, in his place. I wanted a comforting and familiar face above the white collar.

When he asked who the godparents were, I was a little startled. I hadn't even thought about that. But I was even more startled when Rebecca tilted her head at me. "My sister. Miss Annie Martha Revels."

But she hadn't even asked me. I glanced at her, and she gave me a quick, pleading look over the baby's blanket-shrouded head.

On my other side, Mam was nodding and smiling, as if all was going as planned.

I took a deep breath. "That's right," I said to the minister. "I'm George Nathan's godmother."

Nathan cleared his throat. "The godfather's my eldest brother, Tom. He lives down in Charleston, so he can't be here."

I was fascinated; I hadn't even known he had any siblings. Though it never occurred to me before, as much as we had talked about the war, and the water, and each other, I'd never asked Nathan about his family. And it hit me that although I'd thought I knew him, maybe I didn't really know so much. We hadn't had decades together, like Mam and Dad, to learn each other back and front, to make it all seem old news. He'd lived half his life, almost, before we met. Thirty years' worth of Nathan Combs was still a mystery to me, and perhaps would always be so.

We solemnly repeated our parts after Reverend Scarborough. George Nathan was fussing by the time we got to the holy water, and he let out a righteous squall when they tipped him back and sprinkled his head. I heard the congregation chuckle at that, and suddenly I could relax. These people didn't know us and surely had nothing against us. We were all just carrying on with life, and this was one small part of it. So I forgot, while we were up there, to feel nervous. For a while I wasn't even angry at Nathan and Rebecca.

Then we were finished, and the minister directed the congregation to a hymnal page, whatever song Rebecca had chosen. As we filed down the aisle, the pump organ thumped and wheezed to life again, and they sang

> *Eternal Father, strong to save,*
> *Whose arm hath bound the restless wave,*
> *Who bidst the mighty ocean deep*
> *Its own appointed limits keep:*
> *O hear us when we cry to thee*
> *For those in peril on the sea.*

I felt a chill in my joints, and the back of my neck prickled. It was the same song we'd sung over Dad's grave. Why in God's name, with a whole fat blue book of them to choose from, had Rebecca picked that hymn? Before we got to our seats, I wanted to snatch little George from her arms and run out the door with him. To take the boat and run him over quick to the mainland and make sure he never learned to sail or cast a net or drudge an oyster. But the music went on until the sound of it seemed to me evil and endless as a fairy tale curse.

I slipped into my spot in the pew. Then I looked over at Nathan, sitting at the end, on the aisle. And for the first time in ages I stared right at him without looking away, because I saw he was wiping one eye with the back of his hand.

It is wrong, I thought. *All wrong, that hymn.* I felt a fearful shiver for little George and for Rebecca, too. But it was Nathan I felt connected to then, because for a moment, I could see he understood. And sensed the wrongness of it as well as I did.

But I stood through the whole hymn, though I hung my head and kept my mouth shut until, finally, the whole room crooned the last sealing word of doom: *Amen.*

Eleven

After the christening, Nathan came to visit more often, once or twice a week the way he'd done before. Of course, I knew it wasn't me he'd come to see. I had almost begun to believe it wasn't Rebecca, either.

I had always thought men weren't supposed to pay much mind to babies, but Nathan put the lie to that. He was awkward at first, each time he was handed little George, the look on his face was like a man told to juggle a paper sack full of raw eggs. But after a few weeks, he was cradling him in the crook of one elbow like an old grandma. He'd been solemn at the outset, too, staring down deacon-sober at the baby. And little George, in that wide-eyed way new babies have, had stared back, his dark-blue eyes just as serious.

But they soon got over that. By the time the baby was

three months old, he could hold his head up. He was a strong little boy. He liked to laugh and hold on to your fingers and work them like a pump handle. Rebecca, on the other hand, was tired out most of the time now from taking care of him. And Mam had caught cold after our outing to Broadwater, and it hung on and on, the cough lodged deep in her chest. So Rebecca dragged around and complained that Mam wanted things constantly. She said the baby never slept more than two hours at a time and always wanted to suck when he was awake.

"I feel like a wrung-out dishrag," she moaned at breakfast every day.

I was tired, too, but not the bone-melting way I'd been the first year I'd taken over Dad's boat. Now it was nothing to haul in two dozen traps and tong for oysters all morning. I had figured out the quirks and ailments of the boats' rigging, and I knew the channels backward. I was even thinking, down the road, of a new boat, maybe even—though I knew it would have appalled Dad—one with a motor, so I could go farther in a day.

The other watermen hailed me now, or at least nodded if we crossed paths. The previous fall, just a few weeks before the end of the oyster season, I'd rounded the eastern point of Revels Island and there was a codger putting along in an oyster boat, headed my way. As we got closer, I could see he was glaring at me from under his battered hat.

"Black gum against thunder," I whispered to myself, see-ing something of my father in his fierce eyes and the stubborn set of his bearded jaw. *Oh, Dad,* I thought. *If you could see your daughter now.*

Then the fellow seemed to squint and look hard at me again. And as we came abreast and I braced against the rocking of his wake, he raised two fingers off the wheel grudgingly.

So I had been accepted, I guessed, or at least put into a class by myself: *Bless us, thought it was a danged woman in the boat. But it's only that Annie Revels.*

One Saturday morning in September, I watched as Rebecca greeted Nathan at the door. She'd scooped George from my lap at his knock and moved slowly to answer it. I noted how her skin seemed thinner, pulled tight over the bones.

She was wearing a new dress, one she'd sewed up the week before. She'd lost the baby-fat weight and then some, but the dress still didn't suit her. She'd picked out a low-cut pattern, with pleats over the bodice, but her chest had dropped from all the nursing, and it didn't look flattering. She'd trimmed the thing up with lace like a little girl's pinafore. That morning she'd fussed over her hair a good half hour. It looked nice, all brushed and curled, though she'd complained it came out in handfuls in her brush each morning.

She did seem to perk up when she opened the door and saw Nathan standing on the stoop. He stepped inside, leaned over, and kissed little George. But before I turned away, I saw he only patted Rebecca on the cheek. Something squeezed my heart then, but it wasn't pity for my sister.

She handed him the baby and came into the kitchen where I'd just picked up Mam's old wooden spoon to stir the blackberry preserves simmering on the stove. Rebecca waved away the steam that rose from the iron pot. "How can you stand to cook up all this mess in the heat?"

"Cooler now than most days out on the water. Besides, we're almost out of jam, and these berries wouldn't have kept another minute."

She just stood there, fanning, her mouth all screwed up, staring at me.

"What?" I said, skimming foam off the boiling fruit.

She glanced away and sighed. "Maybe you could watch the baby for a little while?"

"Just let me get this into the jars and set them to seal."

I started pouring while she went into the living room. As I was screwing the last lid down, I heard her voice and then Nathan's, raised in some sort of argument. It seemed to be about going off somewhere in the boat.

"You never do. Then what are you here for?" I heard Rebecca shout. But as her voice had gotten louder, his dropped, until I couldn't make out his answers at all. I heard a door slam, and it was quiet again.

I wiped the sticky jars clean and came out to get little George. Nathan was sitting on the couch, holding the baby up under the arms, dancing him in his lap.

"I'm not putting any weight on his legs," he said quickly, when he saw me come in, as though I was about to scold him.

"I know," I said. "It'll give him bowlegs. Rebecca's always on me about not doing that, too."

He laughed. "Once I get one thing right, I start doing something else wrong. Babies are more complicated than a gasoline launch and a steam-powered yacht together."

"Where is Becca? She said she wanted me to watch him a while."

His face reddened. "Oh, never mind about that. I think she's gone down for a nap. I'll take him outside."

Then we were silent a minute. I wanted to move away, and I wanted to stay near him. If he glanced up, I looked away. When I looked up, he turned quickly back to George. I stared at his mouth as he talked to the baby, at the line of his jaw where it darkened with faint stubble. And I recalled suddenly the way the hair on his chest curled around the dark brown circles of his nipples, how it dipped in a sharp V below the waist of his pants. Soon I realized I was wringing the life out of the dish towel in my hands.

We were never alone together anymore. We weren't really alone right then, though there was only Mam in the corner, fiddling with her tatting bobbin and humming her eternal, infernal song, "Leave Her, Johnny."

I excused myself and went back in the kitchen to check the jam jars. They were sealing right nicely, so I moved on to the shed, shut off the gas motor, and cranked a load of wash by hand through the wringer to get my mind off what I couldn't have. I heard the back door of the house open and shut, and I cranked away as if my life depended on it.

As I finished the second load, I glanced out the shed doorway and over the loaded basket I saw Nathan, sitting out on the grass in the shade, under the tree where the other end of clothesline ran from the house. He'd put George down naked on a quilt, to kick his bare little legs in the air. I shoved sweaty strands of hair from my face, feeling annoyed. Had he set up there on purpose? The other side of the house would have been just as good.

I balanced the heavy basket on one hip and went out. I crossed the yard and started pegging wet things to the line. I had my back to them, but I could feel Nathan watching.

As I pinned up the last diaper, he called, "Annie, wait a minute. I want to tell you something."

I dropped my arms to my side. I was sure I didn't want to hear it, especially not right then. But when I turned around and looked at him, my feet moved me on over and I sat on the edge of the quilt. I leaned down, not looking at Nathan, and tickled George's bare belly.

Well, I was sorry right away.

Nathan said, "Last time I did that, he wet me down good, too."

"Oh, Lord," I said, mopping at my lap. My only brassiere was on the line, and it had been too hot to wear an undershirt. Now, looking down as I blotted with a corner of the blanket, I could see my nipples showed through the thin cloth. I dropped the damp blanket and crossed my arms over my chest.

"What is it you want to tell? I need to go change."

"You don't have to," he said. "You know I'd never touch you if you didn't want. No matter how much I'd like to." Then he pressed his lips into a thin line, heaved a sigh. "Ever wonder what it'd be like to die and start over?"

I felt like all the air suddenly leaked out of me. That nothing was holding me up but an invisible string from the top of my head to the sky. I had to keep that string tight, or I'd fall down on the quilt right at his feet. I'd crawl over and lay my head in his lap. I'd push the baby out of the way to do it.

So I hugged my own arms against myself, tighter, until I could feel my nails digging thin new moons into my palms. "Tell away," I said in a ragged voice. "I got to get inside."

He blinked a couple times and looked off over my shoulder. "I been thinking. I could get a job in Charleston. My brother owns half of a stable there, it's a going thing. They take rich tourists around in buggies to see the sights. I'd make more money there. Maybe enough to bring Rebecca and the baby down—"

I opened my mouth to protest, but he held up a hand.

"It'd be enough so I could send you some, too. You wouldn't have to go out on the water."

I felt insulted, first. "What makes you think I don't want to?" I felt the heat of an angry flush spreading over my face. "Marrying into the family don't make you my keeper, Nathan Combs."

He flushed, too, and looked down. "Well, then, you could hire someone to look after your mam."

But as I understood he really meant it, about leaving here, a strange noise rose, a howl like a black wind in my head. Nathan must not have heard, because he went on, still looking away from me.

". . . anyway, I think it would be better for everybody."

And then he did look at me, waiting for an answer.

What have we done, I thought. *And what will I do now?*

I opened my mouth to say something, but no sound came out. Or maybe I answered, but the black roaring was so loud I couldn't hear my own voice.

"Annie." He leaned closer, frowning. "You all right?"

I could smell him then, clean and sharp. And something new: The heavy sweet-molasses-and-malt of whiskey on his breath. Did he have to take a drink, now, to come here?

Then the noise stopped, just like that. I closed my mouth and took hold of the quilt on either side of me, bunching it up in my fists. "No," I said. "I'll never be all right again. *No.*" More hot wetness, dripping on my dress. Running down my cheeks, hitting my shoulders, the front of my already damp dress.

Little George was dry and asleep, thumb sliding from his lips. Oblivious to it all.

Nathan rose to his knees. He took hold of my shoulder with one hand, and with the other drew a handkerchief from his pants pocket. He moved it toward my face, slowly, as if he was trying not to startle a wild animal. He wiped my cheeks and my chin and even my forehead, though that was the one place that didn't need it. It was so much like the first time we met, out there on the water near Steamer Island, when he'd cleaned the blood and dirt off my face with his nice starched white shirt, that I couldn't stand it. Something cracked and broke up inside my chest.

"Please," I said, not meaning a word. "Please don't."

Nathan dropped the wet hanky and grabbed my other arm so tight it hurt. That was why I opened my mouth, to cry out at the hurt, that's all. But he stopped the cry with his mouth. So no sound came out after all, my cry went into him instead, and then we kissed so hard I cut my lips on his teeth or mine, I couldn't tell which, I didn't care.

Then he shoved me away a little, but still leaned close, mumbling in my ear, still gripping my shoulders and giving me a little shake every so many words as if to make me mind him like a child. Jumbled words like, "See? You see, this is why I can't stay. Have to go. Someplace far. Just away."

I could hear now that he was crying, too, which shocked me. I'd never heard a man cry before. My father never had, at least not in front of us. Maybe I didn't think a man could cry, until then.

I felt calmer finally, when his grip slackened, and then he let go.

"Rebecca." he said. "I don't like to stay, because I don't . . . I don't want to be with her."

I should have clapped a hand to his mouth to stop the words. But I didn't; I wanted him to tell me more.

"I stay here sometimes because of him," he said, looking away from me and down at little George. "And it's the only way to be near you, now."

I covered my face with my hands, but really I wanted him to go on. And he did.

"She's angry at me all the time because . . . she knows that." He swallowed and shook his head. "My fault. I can't fix it."

I looked at little George again. Such a helpless scrap of flesh to have so much power over three grown people. Nathan pulled his hand slowly away from my lips. I reached out and took it back. I raised it again, turned it over in my own, and kissed the lined center of his palm. Then I got up and walked back to the house. It was hard to get up and go, but once I did, I felt like running.

Oh, it was wicked, but I wanted to laugh all the way to the door.

A squall blew up in the afternoon, and Nathan stayed. After dinner, Rebecca asked me to keep the baby in my room. I said I didn't mind. It was true, now. I refused to consider yet that Nathan might truly be set on moving away. How could he, when I knew that he still cared for me so much more than her? I thought somehow I would change his mind, make him see that it was best for all of us if he stayed here. It makes no sense now, but that night it seemed to me then I hadn't lost as much as I'd feared.

Little George was fretful, but Rebecca nursed him in my room while I sang him songs in my best passable voice. His eyelids were drooping when she laid him in his basket, which we'd moved to the top of my chest of drawers.

"Well, he's eating his white bread, isn't he," she said, tucking the covers around him.

It was a funny old phrase I'd never really understood before. But now, looking at George, I thought I did. He was content with his warm milk and a soft bed. His needs were as simple as that, and being taken care of by his folks.

"Nice to be a child. Not have to worry about worse than the next treat or toy," she said to me, still looking down at her son. "Remember how that was?"

But before I could think on it or even answer, she turned and said, "Come get me if he wakes up hungry later." Then she left my room.

I meant to think about what she'd said, for it seemed to me it all hadn't been as simple as that. But I fell asleep early, too, tired out from catching up on housework. Perhaps I wasn't happy, in the strictest sense, but I didn't feel as bad as I had earlier. Who knows why? What I had thought I wanted most in the world was fixing to leave me. There appeared to be no way I could ever have Nathan again, the thing that had seemed to me at that moment to be my greatest desire. But that's human nature, something we all need to struggle hard against: the times when you feel the best about what you don't have, because you know that at least someone else doesn't have it, either.

I went to sleep, instead. And dreamed of Granny Jester. She sat up in a big, high, white bed, her glasses glinting like two silver moons. When she screamed, people brought her things. Everyone waited on her: me, Rebecca, Mam, even my dead father. But the things we brought weren't what she wanted, and she threw them back at us. We made piles all around the bed, but still she opened her mouth in a huge scream, a black hole in her face that I thought would swallow me up. Finally, no sound came out, but there was that hole still in front of me, like the pit, like Hell.

I woke up sweating and found I was not in bed, though I had never in my life sleepwalked, even as a child. At least, I saw, I was still in my own room, standing in front of little George's wicker basket, propped on the chest. The room was all but dark, and the odds and ends stacked against the walls threw weird shadows. I wasn't frightened, I was used to the pantry after all the months that had passed since I moved from my old room. All its creaks and dark corners were familiar by then. The one thing I had feared, moving in, was Granny's ghost.

Sometimes when I was still young, I'd think I saw a white flash, the tail of her nightgown disappearing around a corner. Or the glint of her glasses, but it would always turn out to be something else, moonlight on window glass.

A shadow. She had never really bothered me again while I was awake, not since that day I'd seen her ghost standing behind the screen door, waiting for me. For years and years, up until this night, she hadn't even looked at me in dreams with her blank gray spectacles.

It startled me that I had walked in my sleep, traveled somewhere else from my bed all helpless and unknowing. But what frightened me bad was when I looked down and saw the baby's sleeping face, and understood I was standing there over his basket, in the middle of the night, a pillow raised, clutched tight in my two hands.

I threw the pillow away from me and rushed blindly out and through the kitchen, banging my hip on the corner of the table. I stumbled through the living room and down the hall. Stood outside the door of my old room, now theirs, and raised a hand to knock up Rebecca and Nathan. But then I hesitated, my knuckles an inch from the familiar wood. Finally, I lowered my fist and backed away.

I couldn't imagine opening my mouth to say to either one of them, *Come get your baby right now. Before I do it some dreadful harm.*

I walked away, back into the dim parlor, feeling my way through the room. I sat in Dad's old chair, drew my bare feet off the floor, and laid my forehead against my knees.

Was I a woman who could do away with a helpless child, just to gain my own desires? Could I hold a pillow over my own nephew's face in the dark of night as he slept, and then in the light of morning mourn and cry over his cold body?

I groaned, my mouth pressed against a wad of my cotton gown to muffle the awful sound.

Then I heard a rustle, and a big, dark shape raised itself off the divan across from me. I fairly choked on a scream. It wouldn't have surprised me at that moment if it had been the devil himself talking to me. But it was Nathan's low voice.

"What, what's wrong? Annie," he said. "That you?"

I couldn't answer for a moment. I nodded, then understood he might not be able to see that gesture in the dimness and whispered, "Yes. It's me. What you doing out here?"

He hesitated, then said, "George is all right?"

I shivered in the warm, close air and rubbed goose bumps from my arms. "Yes, but—"

But what? What could I tell him?

"I think he's waking up. He'll be hungry soon. Maybe you could take him in to Rebecca."

He sighed. "She won't be happy to see me, but aye." He stood and stretched, bare arms and chest glowing faintly in the moonlight through the front window. He was so close, within reach, I had to look away.

"He's in the basket, in my room," I said. I got up from the chair and started for the kitchen, intending to bring George out to him. But Nathan must have thought I'd meant for him to come get the baby. When I leaned over the basket to lift George out, I bumped into him, he was right behind me.

"Oh. Sorry." I scooted away, off to the side, then held the baby up for him to take. Little George whimpered in his sleep.

But Nathan didn't reach for him. He said, "Are you frightened of me now, Annie?" He sounded unsure. Maybe a little hurt.

I had to bite down on my tongue then to keep from laughing like a loon. Afraid of him? No. Not him at all. It was me, walking around at night all unknowing, a pillow in my hands. That was the one to be afraid of.

But I only said, "I'd never be afraid of you."

In the dimness he ran a hand over his face. "Sometimes I thought, if I hadn't . . . I used to wonder if maybe I had happened on you that day, out on the water, and rushed things too fast," he said. He still didn't reach for the baby.

My heart was jerking in my chest. I couldn't suck in near enough air in each breath. "No," I said faintly.

I heard a howl outside the house, and for a moment wondered if it was Granny come back at last. Then another blast rattled the windowpanes, and it was just the wind again, howling for nothing in particular. I wanted to run out and join it.

"I saw you," he said. "Remember, the one day? In the water. Only you didn't know. I was a ways off, had the old man's field glasses, spotting game. But oh my blessed, all

I spotted was you, peeling out of those dirty men's clothes like a moth out of a cocoon.

"Dropped my jaw, you did, and I near about lost the glasses, too. Then you slid into the water naked as a mermaid, floating there in the cove."

"Stop," I said, my breath now coming and going too fast. "Be still," I whispered into the sweet feathery down on little George's head. Then I laid him in the basket again. I was talking to Nathan, but just like earlier that afternoon, outside on the blanket, I wanted him to go on. To say even more.

He leaned on the bureau, his voice gone low, as if he were alone in the room, trying to convince himself of something. "Then I watched your hands slide over your body. You were so beautiful I wanted to dump a whole boatload of New York doctors in the water and go get you right then and there."

He heaved a great sigh, and I thought he was finally finished. But then he said, "I never thought, after I saw the brains and blood of my friends dead in those trenches, that anything would look beautiful to me again. I couldn't think about caring for anything when it could break, be blown to bits right in front of your eyes."

I took a step closer to him.

"So I never thought, right after we did meet, until I knew more, that I would love you." He turned his back to the dresser again and faced me. "So I was afraid, see."

"Of what?" But all I could think was that he had said it. That he loved me.

"Afraid, when I thought about it later. At the lunch picnic, that mayhap I'd scared you off then."

I recalled his crooked smile, the near swagger in his walk as we had returned to the boat. Me stumbling along in his wake, shocked and wondering at what we had just done. Yet he, too, had been afraid? I could barely credit it.

"Frighten me off?" I said. "You'll never do that."

"I guess I see that now. But I thought you'd never be tied down. You didn't need ary thing in this world. Nothing, nobody's hand, to get along."

But hadn't it been plain, how could he not have known? True, I had never asked him for anything. I had admitted at last to myself that I loved Nathan, but then figured if I said so, he might not answer what I wanted to hear. I couldn't bring myself to risk such a small thing, my own pride.

He sat on the bed, his head in his hands. Gripped his hair as if he'd tear it out by the roots. "Then in your own house, in one stupid night," he said, "I tossed it all into the wind." His shoulders shook.

I couldn't stand any more. To keep from losing my mind, I went over and laid him down on the bed, the way he'd done with me at the cove. I kissed him all over, and I didn't stop at that. Oh, no.

Only a person with a cold stone for a heart wouldn't have done the same.

* * *

After a while, I know he got up, for the baby was fretting. He took him and the basket away. I lay still, my eyes closed, and didn't say a word. When I woke again before dawn, alone, I stayed curled up under the sheet, praying to go back to sleep quick and never wake anymore. I lay there a long while until the morning light reddened my closed lids. Until I finally had no choice but to open my eyes and get up and dress and leave my room. And by then, Nathan had gone.

Twelve

When I finally came out of my room that morning, Rebecca was already at the table, nursing little George his breakfast. A mug of coffee steamed before her, and she was chewing on a hunk of toast smeared with the blackberry jam I'd made the day before.

"Morning." I walked around and sat at Dad's place, yawning. I poured black coffee and drank it, and hoped I wouldn't have to say anything else. I wanted to pretend that the night before had been only another one of my dreams, that it wasn't guilt that made me unable to look Rebecca in the eye.

But my sister never said a word, just chewed her toast and flipped through an old movie magazine and ignored me. A gob of jam dripped on her chin, but she didn't wipe it. Just tore another bite from the bread and went to work on it, chewing so hard her jaw creaked. I saw the bluish circles under her eyes. Even from across the table she smelled as if she needed a good wash. Rebecca, who had always been so particular about her appearance, her hair, her clothes. It struck me hard that I had considered my feelings in all this, and then I had considered Nathan's. But when had I ever wondered about damage to my sister's mind and heart? What a fool and a meddler I had been, to think I knew what was best for her and for everyone.

After all my concern with myself, I felt stung with shame. Or perhaps it was remorse. I cleared my throat and considered saying something. Such as, Shall I take Georgie for a while? You can have a minute to yourself, to clean up.

I turned her way but couldn't decide on the words to begin. I cleared my throat again, but she never even glanced at me.

So I looked away again, worried her silence meant she did know what had happened the night before. I prodded that nasty thought as I finished my coffee and found that I was sorry, but maybe not as much as I ought to be. If my sister had wronged me, I had certainly returned the favor; Nathan and I both had. But mainly I still couldn't bear the idea of having to talk. For in the end, after as many words as we cared to throw at each other, what answer to this trouble would there ever be?

It occurred to me there was one thing I could set straight, from the past.

"Becca," I said quickly. "Do you recall Tommy Kellum?"

She frowned over at me. "Tommy, from school? Aye, the bully."

"Did you ever . . . were you maybe sweet on him once?"

She stared at me in astonishment. "On Tommy Kellum? You must be crazy, Annie. He was *your* beau. I wouldn't have had that great lump on a silver tray. Don't make me laugh." She snorted and went back to chewing on toast.

Well, that left my good intentions about confessing the letters seeming suddenly foolish. Rebecca hadn't ever been interested. Poor Tommy. If he had survived the Great War, she'd have laughed at him and his marriage proposal. But I could think of nothing else to offer my sister, save the one subject I could not bring myself to mention: Nathan.

I finally went out, left the silence of the house, and mercy, the wind was stiff. Looked like a bad blow picking up, much worse than the squall the day before. All the water was whitecapped, the waves had beat up foam on the beach like marshmallow icing. I doubled the lines on the trawler and stowed away the loose gear. Looked at the sky again and wished we had some way of knowing. A phone would have been a help to us, that much of a link to the mainland. The Coast Guard had had one on Cobb's for years. But that was a luxury for most on these islands, and anyway, it would have cost a good deal of money. I sighed to think how much. No chance of that any time soon.

There hadn't been a really bad storm since the terrible

nor'easter back in 1897, and then a nasty storm and flood in the summer of 1903. I had been only two at the time, and couldn't recall a thing. But I'd heard the story often enough from my parents. Even Hog Island went underwater that time, and we'd had to leave Yaupon for higher ground on the mainland. Just as we'd reached the shore, my father told me, he'd seen my mother cry out and point to the east. There was a ship gone on the beach, rolling and yawing in the surf. He'd fought our own craft in as we watched the Lifesaving Service shoot a line to the crew and launch a surfboat. But later they'd heard most had perished in the breakers.

I checked all the lines and made a few extra hitches, shivering with each cold gust. The muggy heat of the night had gone; suddenly early September felt as cool as the tail end of fall. No one would be out on the water today. As I walked back up to the house, a light rain began to fall. The sky above was a uniform gray, as if one big cloud had been stretched tight and tacked corner to corner.

Chickens scrabbled over the marl path before me, clucking anxiously, claws kicking up bits of white shell. Now and then a gust would pick one of the birds off the ground, like a feathered toy. Our two rangy spotted hogs were nowhere in sight. I supposed they'd already scooted away up to the middle of the island, into the scrubby woods where the highest ground lay. They had always been mighty skittish of storms.

Should probably close the shutters now, I thought. But that always made it so gloomy inside, and it meant Rebecca and I would be shut up in a dark box together. I decided to wait for a while. It felt glum enough in there already. I picked up an empty tin feed pail lying by the stoop and set it inside the door.

Rebecca was gone from the kitchen table. I thought I'd heard the door to her bedroom close as I passed through the living room. Mam wandered in, yawning, and headed for the low stool in the corner by the stove.

"Want coffee, Mam?" I asked. "Be ready in a blink."

She nodded, then sat down and watched me pour oil into the lamps. She got up as I was putting the can back in the cupboard, and shuffled over. I noticed she didn't have socks or slippers on. Her bare feet looked bluish white and delicate, the veins standing out. Only the nails appeared tough, ridged and yellowed, the most aged-looking part of her. We couldn't get her to keep her shoes on now, even in winter.

I smiled at her. "What is it, Mam, need the privy? Best to go before it gets really nasty out there. Where'd you leave your old boots?"

She shook her head, then fumbled in her dress pocket. I felt impatient, thinking she'd lost her tatting bobbin again and we'd have to crawl around on our hands and knees for an eternity looking under all the furniture. But then it seemed she found what she was after, and held her hands out to me, cupped over something.

I put mine out to receive whatever it was, a wad of string

or an old nutshell, but instead she dropped some hard round things that felt cool against my palm. I looked down at two shiny gold circlets.

"Wedding bands," I said, pushing them around with one finger. "But this is yours, and here's Dad's."

She smiled, and closed my fingers over the rings. "For love, maid," she said.

I closed my eyes a moment, then tried to smile. "Too late, Mam."

I tried to hand them back, but she shook her head stubbornly. "Eldest needs them most," she said, folding my fingers back over the rings again. "And I'm done."

I stared at her a moment, wondering if I didn't give her enough credit for taking in what happened around her. What did she know or suspect of the happenings in the house lately? I couldn't say, then or now. I slipped the rings in my pocket, meaning later to put them back in her room, in the little carved box Dad had made. They should be hers as long as she lived; I certainly had no use for them.

Off and on I played with the rings in my pocket as I went about the house. I recalled the night before, how Nathan had said I'd never seemed to need anything or anybody. I worried at that thought all morning. It was true I'd never learned to flirt or act coy as the other girls had at school. As I grew up, I had only the example of Mam and Dad to know how women and men were together. But by then they were already old; easy with each other, kind but distant. They'd not seemed to have much need to talk about things by then, and in the last years they moved mostly in different worlds: she in the house, with Rebecca, he out on the water. And I had chosen his way, or rather it had chosen me.

Except for my father, no man had ever stepped in to show or tell or do for me. If Nathan had known I needed him as much as I'd wanted him, would things have been different? I despaired to think it might be so. But the thought would not leave me alone. Soon he would surely leave for Charleston, or elsewhere, and Rebecca and George would follow. I was sure he'd never abandon them, no matter how he felt about me. Not that men didn't ever do such things, but I knew for a surety Nathan wouldn't. And as much as I might wish it, I knew I couldn't.

The leading edge of the storm came on us fast. First I noticed the tide was higher than I'd ever seen it, lapping over the grass and the beach, though it should have been falling. Yaupon Island was low, even the woods where the hogs hid out wasn't really much above sea level. I wondered if we ought to head over to the mainland, or at least to Hog Island. I rejected the idea of Cobb's. It was larger, too, but barely higher than Yaupon.

And Nathan was there. I wanted so badly to see him, I knew we'd best stay away. So instead I lit the lamps and set them all about the house, to chase the early gloom. Then, as the wind screeched and moaned around the eaves,

I went back outside and latched the shutters. Each gust did its best to wrench them out of my hands, if not off their hinges. And out past the beach, the water rose even higher.

I'd already secured the boats with chains and line, and rolled the old oyster boat's canvas sails up tight and lashed the rudder and the boom. So after one last look around, I fought my way over to the sea side, leaning into the blow, to see how bad things looked there. It took me longer than the usual five minutes, pushing hard against that wind. A few gulls leaned stoically on the topmost spot under a big driftwood branch, tails to the wind. Though I heard a hog snuffle and grunt from the blackberry thicket as I stumbled past, I saw neither bristle nor hoof of them.

What I did see when I got over the rise took the breath out of me.

The beach was gone. Waves pounded the east shore, or what was left of it. They must have been doing so, with greater and greater force, all through the night. In the distance I saw, far out, huge gray breakers charging in rapid succession, some soaring into the slate sky so high I couldn't imagine how big they really were.

I looked down at the beach again. Dad's marker, the big wooden cross we'd had made with his name and dates on it, was gone. At first I wasn't even sure where the grave lay. Then a curling wave withdrew and I saw a depression in the ground. I'd had them dig it close to the waterline to salve my conscience, since I wasn't burying him at sea. Now I saw the oncoming storm had eroded his resting place, so that it looked almost empty. Granny Jester's smaller weathered marker was still in place, but tilted crazily to one side. I couldn't make out the grave of my baby brother at all.

I ran back toward the house, easy to do now since the wind helped too much, lifting me off my feet till I was nearly flying home. As I rounded the corner I thought I heard the rumble of an engine, a ridiculous notion. But then I saw a yellow-slicker-clad figure dragging a long boat up on the inner beach. He threw out one big anchor on the sand, then another, both on heavy lengths of chain. Then he turned back to look at the house. Even before the wind snatched back the hood of his oilskins, I knew it was Nathan.

I met him halfway up.

"Are you crazy?" I shouted. "What're you doing out in this?"

He looked at me and smiled. "What're you doing out in it, eh?" he said, and for a minute I forgot all that had happened since we met over an old oyster boat run aground. I hugged him to me, and then pushed away till we were at arm's length.

He shook his head. "Going to be a bad one, Annie. You should have been gone off here already. I come to carry you all to Cobb's. That's close as we can make it. It's bigger, and the buildings there will hold."

I had to argue that. "We've rode out many a storm right

here over the years. Dad and my uncles built this little house to endure."

But then there was Mam, so frail now.

Nathan shoved his hands in his pockets and looked at me sideways. "I knew you'd not like the idea."

"But?" I said, for I saw he had more to say.

He looked out over the water, then back at me. "But in the eyes of God and all the laws, little George and Rebecca are my lookout. You can't be deciding everything for the three of us now."

I opened my mouth but found in my head no ready answer to that. I had to admit, some of my decisions had not gotten me into the place I'd hoped to be. The way I'd seen it, I had to be the one, had to fill in for Dad. I wondered if Nathan could be right—if I had always just forced my will on them, instead of doing the best thing.

Maybe, I thought, *it would be nice not to be in charge, this once.*

"All right," I said slowly, for it didn't feel natural to me, to let go of deciding things. "All right. We'll get a few things. A couple blankets and some food."

"Not much, mind. We need to go now."

I felt a prickle of irritation at him then. Had I not been born and spent all my life on this water? No fancy bill-hatted guide knew better than I what a storm could do. But he had already come all this way against the blow for us. So I only hesitated a moment, then bit my lip and trapped the hard words I was thinking. I went inside, grabbing slickers. I got one onto Mam, handling her a bit roughly in the process. She didn't complain. I set her on the boot bench by the front door and told her to wait on me. Nathan brushed past, shedding rivers off his oilskins.

"She's in the bedroom," I called after.

"Now you wait here," I said again to Mam.

I followed along to help carry things, but when I got to the door, he and Rebecca were arguing.

"Well, he's my son, too," I heard her say. "You don't want a baby out in such god-awful weather."

"Rebecca," Nathan said. He was leaning there in the doorway as if he wasn't allowed in. I felt baffled at the pleading in his voice. Why didn't he just tell her, as I would, and be done with it?

"It's too dangerous to stay here," he said. "Ground's too low. And I'm only going to load us all up and go as far as Cobb's Island. Why, look. You can stay in a room at the hotel."

She caught sight of me behind him then.

"Ah, sure," she said bitterly. "We'll only need the one bed."

"That's enough," said Nathan, his face turning red with anger. "We're going, now."

He reached into the basket and scooped up George, who was by then adding his loud opinion to the din.

"Put him back," she cried. "Are you going to give her my baby, too?"

Nathan stopped with George hoisted on one shoulder. I

saw his face darken even more, saw him raise a hand and turn back toward her. I thought for one awful moment he was going to hit my sister. I stepped forward, and I know what I would have done if he had harmed Rebecca. But he only grabbed her arm and pulled her on into the hall.

At the front door, Rebecca finally put on a slicker, suddenly docile enough. She scowled at me all the while, though, anger and hatred plain in her look as she went out, Nathan urging her along from behind. He held the wailing baby wrapped in an oilcloth cover from the kitchen table. As we ran toward the boat, I wrapped my arms around Mam's waist and huddled over her, fearing she was light enough now she might actually blow away. Nathan handed Rebecca in, and it was not his old blue skiff, but a big, long, gasoline motor launch, a new one the Cobbs had just ordered and taken delivery on.

"The old man told me to take it," Nathan said, as I helped him push us off. "He thinks this is just another overrated blow. Won't budge from his cottage on the place. But even the Coast Guard has left now. One of the Cobb wives got the others riled up and his sons took them and the kids to the mainland early this morning. The guests all left last night."

"He probably thinks this boat is unsinkable, too," I said, then wished I kept my mouth shut.

"I hope to God it is," said Nathan. "The old man's never been wrong yet."

The launch was certainly loud and fast. It screamed and

pounded through the waves and troughs as it cut a path for us around the south end of Yaupon and northeast across the water toward Cobb's. When we roared out into the unprotected channel between the two islands, it reared like an island pony over huge breakers. Big waves bore down on us and broke across the bow in waterfalls, drenching us as if our slickers were made of paper.

"Head about," I shouted to Nathan. I began to wonder if we shouldn't perhaps turn back. Loaded down as it was, I was afraid the boat would easily capsize. Even a good swimmer wouldn't last long in such a storm.

At first I thought he hadn't heard, but then he looked back at me as if he was mighty annoyed. Finally he wrenched at the tiller, and the boat responded sluggishly. The engine roared and whined, and he pointed her for a deeper patch, where with less shoaling the whitecapped breakers would be less violent. But still the boat rocked and reared.

I looked back at Rebecca, who clutched little George, her face green and sick. But he, in the strange way of babies, was quiet; perhaps lulled by the constant rocking motion. I was most worried about Mam, but when I glanced her way, she was gripping the lines, being tossed limply about like a child's doll. The old girl had a smile on her face as if she was enjoying the wild ride. I recalled then that her gift to me, her rings, must still be in the pocket of my trousers. I hadn't had time to put them away in her room.

Nathan turned east when we got closer to Cobb's. I figured he meant to hug the western face of the island and go around, making for the south side, where it might be easier to pull up the launch on the more sheltered beach at the Guard station. Sheets of rain made the shrubby west-side beach a blur; the sea grass flat as a gray carpet. It must have been a trick of the eye, or my frightened imagination, but as we rounded to the south end of Cobb's, I saw that the flagpole of the station appeared to curve under the assault of the wind.

He must have noted the pole, too, which marked the beach, for just as it came into view, Nathan wrenched again at the tiller to turn her in toward shore.

It was too soon, I saw.

His eyes were fixed on the shore; he seemed distracted from the idea that danger could still come at us from the west, from behind. Yes, I saw he'd turned us too soon, and not only that, he wasn't coming about sharp enough. If we were caught midships by one of the bigger waves, it'd swamp us sure.

I thought then to simply grab the tiller from him and cut it sharper, to help. I'd fought my share of storms before out on the water, making a run for it after a day's work. I knew I could do the job right. But even as I decided this, he glanced back at me, as if he knew my very thoughts. So instead I hesitated.

What made me stay my hand was this: I saw he knew I wanted to take over. The face he turned my way was mostly a wet blur, washed by rain and contorted with the effort of holding our course. But his gaze was piercing and wary.

Was I so stubbornly predictable? That stung me, and I suppose it might be that I hesitated the way a wife might, to give him time to save face and manage the situation. But what I fear is that somewhere in a dark, unnatural corner of my heart, I coldly decided to give in, to seem to need his help, and let him do this one thing straight through. Then, mightn't there not be some way I could still have Nathan, even yet?

So I didn't reach for the tiller.

Instead, I put my faith in God, and in Nathan's judgment, and prayed we were nearly safe, as the launch wallowed in a trough and slowly, slowly came about. Nathan aimed the bow at the south beach, what little could be seen of it. And I prayed as I had not in years.

As I did, I turned and looked behind us.

Less than a hundred yards off, a huge wave was bearing straight for the launch. As it curled to come down on us, I saw it carried all sorts of weeds and flotsam and some debris: pieces of somebody's barn, or maybe a shed. Then a giant's fist made of splintering wood and crushing water hit us, shoving the boat on its bow down, almost on its beam ends, all but capsizing it.

Rebecca slammed against me, knocked my breath clean away. I heard Nathan shout something, and I tried to draw breath to answer. But I sucked up water instead of air. For a moment it seemed there was nothing but a tornado of wind and water all around me. Then I saw Rebecca again, her mouth wide in a scream, one arm flailing. She seemed to be clawing her way across the tilted deck toward me, clutching little George to her with her other arm.

When she had reached out for me on Dad's work boat, that time she was three and almost drowned, I had taken her hand. Just the year before, at Dad's grave, I had reached out again, and clasped her outstretched hand in mine, loving her then as my sister, my nearest, dearest kin. But this time, I turned away.

I turned from Rebecca to look first for Nathan. And saw the wheel was spinning crazily, abandoned. Then the boat tilted again, revolved like a child's toy in a bathtub. I understood we had been driven aground on a bar, and that the waves would soon pound us to pieces. I clutched at the bench seat and hauled myself upright again, my boots slipping on seaweed and water.

Only then did I wonder, where was Mam?

"Annie," shouted Rebecca's voice, somewhere near my ear. I pushed water and hair from my face and saw that she'd been thrown back against the stern and was clinging there. She reached out again, and as the boat was rocked by yet another breaker, I lunged toward her. Clutched her wet fingers, grasped them for a moment.

I knew Rebecca could swim, though not well. But the baby—

I let go of her hand and pulled him from her arms. And then, as the bow heaved up a final time in the hard surf, it flung my sister out. I saw her shocked white face like a ghostly mask hung for a moment in the air. Heard what I thought must be her last sound on this earth, a high scream. Or else the terrible sound I heard was Granny Jester come back to me again, for a moment, to point out all my mistakes, with the same outraged cry she'd made leaving this world before she was ready.

Then the wind and water tore Rebecca away.

I gripped the sodden bundle that was little George tight in my arms as we slid across the canted, splintering deck, my rubber boot soles screeching and skidding on oiled teak. The whole launch dove under a new wave and then I was in the salt, too, gagging as it jammed a wet hand down my throat. I clawed for a grip on a splintered chunk of plank and kicked like mad, trying to keep my head and the baby's above water. I heard him gasp and choke, and knew at least he hadn't drowned.

The waves sent the both of us reeling and bobbing like an untethered fishing float. We were in the water and battered about for some while. I lost sight of the shore, or any mark of it, even the spire of the flagpole. But at last, as if tired of an old game, the waves shoved us roughly onward, as if bent on either killing or saving. Surf crashed and boomed around us, and finally slammed us down onto what was left of Cobb's sandy beach. I crawled a ways, collapsed, then dragged us both up a little farther, out of the shallows. I rose on hands and knees and looked back, but no one else dragged out of the breakers.

"Nathan," I called, my throat scratched raw from the salt water. "Rebecca? *Mam!*"

All I heard was surf crashing on the shore, the hurricane shrieking like a mad flying beast overhead. I hugged the baby to my chest and thought he was crying, though it might have been my own sobs I heard. My boots were gone, my slicker wrenched halfway off. I stumbled over broken shells and rubble, shoved one way then another by the wind, tearing my bare feet on sharp driftwood bits, planks with nails.

It seemed the wild currents had carried us around the island a ways, for I didn't see the Coast Guard station in front of us. So I looked for the hotel, for the sturdy board-walk that led to it over the dunes.

That was the next shock. The broad, cedar-shingled roof of the three-storied building, which I should have been able to see easily over the low myrtle bushes and dwarfed, wind-stunted pines, was gone. Only a few upright timbers, pitiful as broken sticks from a child's forgotten play, jutted into the air.

The Guard station was farther down the beach, I de-cided, into the teeth of the wind, but I turned that way. I was too afraid of what else I might find in the ruins of the hotel. To the north all I could see was the flagless drill pole, so I set my sights on that and stumbled on. At some point I picked up a length of rope the wind was skittering along the sand, lively as a snake. I meant to tie the baby to me for safekeeping, but first I hoped to find Nathan, or Mam, or Rebecca. Surely I couldn't be the only one left.

I bent double, gasping and fighting to move on, while the tide kept playing with me, rolling strange obstacles in my path. A wagon wheel, a dead mule, a child's toy piano that made wet clinking and plinking sounds before it was whisked off by the next wave. Then, as I neared the station, a huge breaker crashed in, bearing a body. I rushed over, and saw waterlogged trousers, a yellow slicker.

"Nathan!" I cried, and, hugging little George to me with one arm, I bent and grabbed a handful of rubber slicker to turn him over. Drowned sightless eyes stared up, but the hair was white, and a long beard covered most of his face: Old Man Cobb. Why had Nathan listened to the old fool? He had been wrong about everything. The hotel, the boat, everything. I slammed my fist down on his lifeless chest, but it only made a dull wet smack that was not enough, not nearly enough.

So I grabbed hold of his slicker and jerked him upright. What I shouted at his poor battered body I don't recall. No words would bring me Nathan again, or my mother or sister. My grieving, fear-addled mind had to admit that at last, and I let the old man drop back into the shallow surf. I rose and dragged on across the sand, toward the station.

In the end, I stumbled over it. First I saw a lone wooden desk, pushed by the wind, skating back and forth inside the scoured foundation like a skittish horse in a stall. I whimpered when I finally understood that that was it; this blasted ruin was all the storm had left me. Then I staggered back to the drill pole and leaned against it, buttoning the baby snug inside my slicker. I decided I'd better lash us tight to the pole. I did it right clumsily with numb white fingers, and hoped the loose, ugly knots would hold.

"They'll come for us soon, Georgie," I whispered. "You'll see."

I hugged him close to keep him warm. Hunched my shoulders and bent my head against the chill. Maybe soon someone would come looking. Yes, maybe even Nathan would appear, walking up the beach grinning, his arms around Mam and Rebecca. I wanted that more than anything, just to see his face, alive and smiling, even if I never got to touch or hold or speak to him again after this day.

I told George from time to time that help was sure to be here soon. I knew he couldn't understand, so it was as much to reassure me as him. But after a few hours had passed, I knew that it was unlikely. I was all-over numb by then. My arms had first set in to tingling, then aching, till at last they were just dead, senseless sticks. But I wouldn't let go of little George. I rocked him a bit, and croaked hoarse froggy sounds meant to be lullabies. He was my nephew, perhaps by then my only living kin. And he was Nathan's baby. What would I say to him if anything bad happened to his son?

I had plenty of time to think, though I believe at times

I slept, too. *Surely I could have tried harder to save Becca. If only I had taken the tiller from Nathan. Should I untie the rope now and go search the beach?* I woke once from a bad dream of choking underwater, and saw the blowing rain and gray blur of surf before me. I wondered where I was, then felt Georgie, and the ropes that still held us. And wept because it hadn't been only a nightmare after all.

The sky grew even darker, and the wind still howled, though not as loudly. Sometime during the night the baby began to whimper like a kitten, and I knew he must be hungry. But what did I have to give? Finally I could stand his mewing cries no more. I reached under my slicker, unbuttoned my shirt, and pressed his face to my breast. I felt his mouth fumble at me, felt him suck weakly for a moment. Then he let go and I thought, *That's good. Better if he sleeps till help arrives.*

Much later, the wind died to a low moan. Between ragged black scraps of cloud the stars came out and seemed to wheel around me, bright as pinpricks in a tin lantern.

"Look, Georgie," I whispered through salt-cracked lips.

By then he was much too quiet. I worried that he had died of the wet and the cold. That mayhap I'd smothered the tyke, pressing him too close to my body. I tried not to recall the night I'd sleepwalked to his basket and stood there, a pillow clutched in my hands. The thought was too terrible to bear.

"No," I said and shook that picture out of my head, hard.

I crooned all sorts of nonsense to keep Granny away. I sang old ballads and silly songs, but no lullabies.

Finally, when he still didn't move, I slipped a hand inside my slicker and stroked his little arm, petted the wet down on the top of his head. He felt cold, even to my chilled fingers, and he didn't move under my hand or make any sound.

"Don't you fret. I won't let go," I said, pulling him close again.

I was still holding little George the next morning, when the sun came up bloody red over a calm sea. I didn't turn loose of him even when, far down the beach, some watermen pulled a skiff up and walked around, caught between marveling and cursing in loud voices at the damage. My legs were so weak I'd slipped down the drill pole long since, and was sitting with my back propped against the base, so I suppose they didn't see me at first. My bad knots had held, all right. It was me who had given out.

I heard their voices coming nearer and tried to call to them. All I could make by then was a low rasping sound, the cawing of a worn-out crow. They started, looked all about, then rushed over my way, stumbling over debris. They had to cut the wet knotted rope to get me loose and carry me to the skiff.

But when they tried to take Georgie, I clawed and fought like a weak mother cat.

"Missus," said a stocky, redheaded man finally. "Please, missus, let us help. Your poor baby's dead."

I wouldn't listen. Was sure they lied.

At last they relented and let me hold his body all the way back.

*As we crossed the water and rounded the point again toward Yau-*pon, gradually I saw the state of our place. Both boats were wrecked, the bar cat lying on its starboard side in the front yard. A lone chicken perched forlornly on top of the splintered railing. As for the dock, a few pilings still jutted from the water like crooked teeth in a jaw. The toolshed lay canted on its side.

Shingles were gone, so the roof had a scabby, abandoned look. One broken front window looked darker than the others, forbidding as an empty eye socket. But when I wept, it was not for all the damage. It was because, in the midst of all that ruin, our house still stood, safe, whole, and of a piece on Yaupon Island.

Thirteen

The next morning, the Coast Guard brought me word Mam's body had washed ashore at Cobb's. They'd taken her to be laid out at Hog Island, mistaken for some poor woman gone missing there. The idea of strangers handling my mother's body would have bothered me a good deal once. It didn't matter so much by then. I'd already seen that Dad's grave had been hollowed by the storm; his coffin washed away. He'll spend his eternity with the sea after all.

Little George lay in his basket in my old room. I'd gently washed and dried his body and wrapped him in Mam's best linen tablecloth, the only one left whole from her wedding trousseau. I was determined to wait for the minister this time. A baby needs every inch he can gain, I figure, in this world and the next.

I tried hard not to think too much about Nathan or Rebecca, so of course I thought of them all the time.

Just after noon the same day, another boat arrived. I was sitting up in Dad's chair, my feet wrapped in rag bandages. It still hurt like the devil to stand, but I hobbled to the door. I saw a burly waterman, whom I finally recognized as young Sam Doughty under a new beard he must've grown since summer's end. He was carrying a bundle, long and awkward, like a body wrapped in a blanket. I closed my eyes, afraid to look, afraid not to. I backed away, and he brought the bundle inside.

He laid it gently on the sofa, and pulled a corner of the blanket away. There was Rebecca's face, her hair like dark, tangled seaweed. Her skin dead pale, as if all the blood had drained away, looking all the more white for a purplish egg-shaped bruise on one cheekbone. I pushed a fist into my mouth and shook my head, because although I had thought up till then my sister must have perished, I hadn't yet imagined what it would be like to look on her empty shell.

Then she turned her head and coughed, and I was down on my knees at her side, the pain in my body and legs and feet forgotten. I groped in the blanket for one of her hands and took it and chafed it, trying to make her warm. The icy feel of her skin chilled me, despite the good fire that burned a few feet away from us.

"Found her halfway over to Parramore. Pulled her out the water myself," Sam Doughty said. "Damn nor'easter drug her clean to kaflugie. But she had a grip on some timbers. Had to pry her fingers loose even then."

He leaned over suddenly and took her other hand, cradled it like a small, delicate animal in his big, sun-browned ones.

"She's a strong little thing," he said.

I hesitated a moment, having never in my life thought of my sister that way.

"Yes," I said slowly, rubbing tears and snot from my face. "Yes, she must be."

He stayed a while. Told me how he'd laid her in the stern boards and run it full tilt to the doctor over in Wachapreague. Where he found the waiting room full, so he'd stayed and waited. When I asked if I might reimburse him for all that, he looked offended, so I quickly let that subject drop.

He promised to bring back Mrs. Killmon over later from Hog Island, to help out. "She was mighty broke up about the little one. Said she hasn't lost but one she delivered before, and that was to breakbone fever."

"No sign of any others?" I asked, still rubbing Rebecca's hand. I would boil water, make some tea or broth, and spoon it up to her until she was warm and stronger. "There's my brother-in-law, Nathan Combs—"

"No'm." He twisted his hat round in his hands and shook his head. "At least, none that's yet living." He glanced back over his shoulder through the open door. "See your boat came through right well. You need ary hand with it this fall, just ask."

He shuffled his feet at the door a bit, then sighed.

"Well," he said. "Better turn to." And he then was gone up the path and back to the water.

Rebecca was taken with a fever that night, gasping for breath, and Mrs. Killmon feared it was pneumonia. She dosed her with horehound tea and camphor and molasses and wrapped her heaving chest in an onion poultice. I sat by her bed all night, expecting to lose her. In the early hours before true dawn, I decided I'd give anything to have her well and whole. I would bury Georgie and Mam with my bare hands and not mourn for Dad's body. I'd give up a whole life's worth of going out on the water just to see her open her eyes and know me again.

I had plenty of time to recall when we were little and played together, and how often I had been mean and spiteful to her. I burned with shame to remember the way I'd hated her at first for taking my place, as the baby. And because when we had gotten older, I'd hated her again, for no reason other than she got so much praise for her looks. It struck me that I didn't really know Rebecca at all. Like Nathan, I had mostly made her up and been satisfied with my own vision. Then I had tried to move them all to my will, and some ways made a terrible, terrible mess of it.

I sat by the bed and held her hands, still trying to warm them. I struggled to pray and found it hard, hard, for I had so fallen out of the habit. But by dawn, I decided I would give up going out on the water to stay home and take care of her. I understood, at last, that I had chosen to head our family, to provide for her and Mam; they had never asked it of me.

And I decided I would willingly give up, even in the farthest reaches of my heart, the least claim on Nathan Combs. If by some miracle he still lived and walked in our door right then, I would have willingly turned away and sent him on to Rebecca. If I marveled at these new thoughts in the dark, it was only at how easy it was to push away what I'd once thought my two greatest desires.

In the morning, Rebecca was some better. I don't believe it had more to do with my promises and prayers than with Mrs. Killmon's constant nursing and strong remedies. But I felt as if I could claim some hand in her progress, all the same. She wasn't well enough to go to Mam and Georgie's funeral, of course, though we had a surprising turnout of folks from as far as Hog Island, nearly a dozen. Even a couple of Cobbs showed up, looking like ordinary island folk, and were not at all unfriendly.

So now, six months after the storm, my sister is holding on, though she still isn't strong. It seems she takes a chill or cough at the least change in the weather. The doctor tells me all that exposure during the storm and the seawater in her lungs has weakened her constitution. "Just broke it right down," he says.

He also says he doubts she'll live out the next year. But I aim to prove him wrong there.

"She's not broken," I told him. "It's just, sickness and grief have taken all the good she had in her and sucked it right up. She'll come around in due time."

He often shakes his head as he closes up his black bag but still smiles at me when he leaves. Sometimes even an educated man is smart enough to know that all the answers aren't in books.

If Rebecca recalls much of the storm or the sinking of the launch and the moment I pulled the baby from her before she went overboard, she hasn't said. At first I wanted to bring it up, to tell my side of it. But that would be pure selfishness, I understand that much at least. Still, when she is awake and looks at me now, I watch for signs. Doubt, accusation. If she smiles at me, I feel such relief. If not, I worry: *What is it that she is remembering?*

It's not that I think I'm so important the Lord has singled me out, like Job. We all played our parts in this story and, except for poor little George, made our choices and our mistakes, too. Still, I want to understand it all. Most nights I can tell myself I chose the baby because he was helpless; my nephew, my sister's child, our own blood. Other times I am overcome again with shame, because I sometimes worry that the true reason I snatched him could be different. He was, after all, the only part of Nathan I had a chance to save for myself.

Lately, Sam Doughty has been coming by regular, too. First thing, he always checks on my boat-repairing progress. Usually he brings gifts, practical ones like fittings and paint and varnish; things he knows another waterman will appreciate.

Then I always lead him inside, to Rebecca's place by the fire where she sits in Dad's old chair, wrapped in a quilt. On a good day she might be awake and smile at him. If she's sleeping, he always takes up one of her small white hands in his large sun-browned ones, as he did when he brought her home to me. And then he says, like an incantation or a prayer, "She's a strong little thing." But he sounds less amazed now and more hopeful.

For his sake and my own, I always agree. I have seen the interest in his eyes when he gazes at my sister. It's not simply the satisfied, benevolent look of a savior but something more complicated, more fragile and human.

They never found Nathan's body. Three months ago, I sent a letter to his brother in Charleston, but I didn't have any real address, so I don't know if it arrived. I never received any reply.

I'm sure Nathan is dead, but nonetheless I like to imagine him living down in some other far-off place. Charleston is as good as any. He is well and smiling and has a new uniform on. He wears a different kind of hat now, too, and takes the tourists out in a fancy carriage drawn by two sleek bays. He knows everything about the town; things the visitors would never even think to ask. He has the deep tan of a man who spends most of his time outdoors and a faraway look in his eyes. And sometimes, though he wouldn't actually do it, he imagines traveling north.

That's just my own daydream, of course. I know a living Nathan would never go away and leave his family, or me for that matter, unless God and nature insisted on it.

I'm grateful for the part of our family that remains. I have no plans to leave or to live anywhere but Yaupon Island the rest of my days. It hasn't been long enough yet not to miss the others every day: Mam, Georgie, Nathan. But despite all grief and bad weather, we've gotten this far. So I don't try to imagine what the future might hold. I don't dream of marriage, or a husband, or children of my own. But who knows? I wear Mam and Dad's wedding rings on a string around my neck now. I am content to wait and see what comes.

Now, when I spot the black line of a coming squall to the west, it looks to me like the approaching army of an old, indomitable enemy. And when I look seaward, the new markers in our little graveyard beyond the house remind me of all our mistakes. But someone must put flowers on little George's grave, and straighten and mend the crosses, and feed Rebecca and brush her hair. When this winter is over, I've promised to wash and comb it out in the sunshine.

To live on the Shore, you must understand that good

weather often follows close after bad. Some folks will say that the nor'easter of 1920 was a curse, or a punishment, or a judgment on us. But I am my father's daughter, and a waterman knows the hand of God is never set on crushing us. We weather what comes our way, and in the end it makes us stronger.

So in spring, when Rebecca's better, I'll go out on the water again. It's turning fair already. I'll set new pots and run a mile of trotline. And at the end of the day, when the sun goes down, I'll come back to the house our father built. Its old pine timbers have always held good and true. I know I can count on them to remain stronger, and more enduring, than any beating heart.